THROUGH SHADOW FOREST

A FANTASY NOVEL

SWORD MASTER OF HONEY HEART RESORT

JONATHAN EVAN HUDSON

THROUGH SHADOW FOREST

ROMEO

Romeo knew, he was sure that, crows should only have two eyes, but blink blink blink.

Yes.

It wasn't just eye crust getting in the way.

At the very end of a twisting thick branch of this oak tree, that big fat crow, it definitely had three big beady eyes.

Not two.

A third eye was right in the middle of its forehead. An eye that blinked back at him like the rest of its eyes. It stared intensely at him, like he was an earthworm that bird was eager to snap right up ...

The glare from the pale white moonlight, no mistaking it. The big fat moon cast a bright milky gleam over everything. As if Romeo had spilled milk everywhere again but without Aunt Tilda to yell and wallop him for wasting so much of the precious drink.

As if twenty something was too young to drink proper liquor, so he better still stick with ordinary milk, least according to Aunt Tilda, and since it was her home, so her rules.

But the way the fat crow was perched so tense yet cozy. It was alert, yet still faking some kind of relaxed search, as if it was searching for a stray corpse to feast on. How it bent the end of the thinning end of the thick branch with all its pump weight … how the bend was nearly a pace down.

Far more than Romeo thought it should, blink blink blink. He was blinking but …

Maybe he was just seeing things. He did just wake up from a strange dream he couldn't remember. His eyes were still crustier than one of Aunt Tilda's countless peach pies baked to steaming perfection.

But there was no chance of falling back to sleep now. Not with the crickets wailing like a little chorus of banshees everywhere. The frogs didn't help either. They were screeching their own frantic tunes.

Never mind the grunts and growls of giant beasts below every so often. The hefty huffs and sniff upward. The sounds came from at least halfway to this very branch.

And this branch was at least a dozen paces from the ground.

That hard stone ground.

Occasionally something big and fierce ripped at the moss closer to the bottom of the tree's thick trunk. As if pa were training his blade on the mossy beard of this oak. Or his dwarven grandpa and his beloved doubled edged axe.

But neither his pa or grandpa would attack the deep crack at the bottom. Shaking the whole tree a touch like the massive creatures below were doing occasionally.

Despite how thick and sturdy the tree was.

Then again, no one ever thought sleeping in Shadow Forest was a good idea. It just happened to be the only decent option for now.

Sort of.

He simply enjoyed the naturally rosy fragrance of Vivian as she slept soft and cozy, her back against his chest. Her sultry body sent his heart thumping louder than any cricket screech. Faster than any frantic frog cry. She was using him like the back of a loveseat, and honestly, he couldn't be happier for it.

Even here. As dangerous as Shadow Forest was at night.

And another reason that crow at the end of their branch ... Romeo better be extra cautious. It might not just be him it was eying for a snack.

No. Not just might.

Vivian was, as the dime dreadfuls would say, curved slim in the right spots, curved ultra-fat in the chest spots. Her long rosy pink hair softened her back pressing against him. His leather vest was wide open as he hugged her slim waist, her slim stomach snuggly. His crotch against her fine, fine ass, even with his trousers on, as Vivian had insisted.

Her breathing, slow and sleepy steady, unlike his racing happy heart.

Her grip, hugging his arms around her snug and tight.

But she wasn't defenseless.

Far from it.

Her leotard of pink with suggestive white hearts, along with her thigh boot sandals and fingerless elbow gloves and their guards all protected her, and magically too. From ordinary weapons and even some defense against magical weapons.

All because she was a clawgirl. A monster of legend so to speak, even if she was in her human form right now. She hadn't yet showed him her reptilian form. Not yet.

But he knew her skin could become scaly like a serpent and even more protective than her human skin, which, technically, was actually very, very fine scales that only looked and felt like human skin. Her hands and feet could go taloned like a reptile too and she could wield special powers with them.

But she hadn't yet revealed her clawgirl form to him—yet.

She must not want him to think less of her. As if he would. They spared forever at Honey Heart Resort, a resort they both worked at. Putting on a show for patrons, but of course, Romeo was always required to lose. Vivian always required to win—until some handsome rich patrons tried his luck and defeated her while she always went down as sexy and sultry as she could.

And wow, could Vivian go sexy sultry.

But just yesterday, she had been slaved into fighting as a proper clawgirl was meant to, against humanity, and they had fought for real.

Until he freed her with a ... perverted kind of purifying attack.

Thankfully her archer garb somehow recovered after a while as well, or else she so could have clonked him good, as he would have deserved.

Yet ... Romeo knew monsters of legend were real now, and yes, he had heard of three-eyed crows somewhere before ... but where ... where had he heard of three-eyed crows before ...

Good thing Vivian had her pair of pink scimitars. They were hanging sheathed off her thick belt. They could easily be snapped together by the pommels to form a bow that could fire magical steel bolts as long as her stamina lasted.

And did Vivian had some good stamina.

Romeo wasn't unarmed either. His harpe was a powerful magical crescent blade with a razor-sharp inside. Able to slice through the hind and armor of monsters of all sorts.

Even the protective scales of a clawgirl.

If need be.

But hopefully ... never again. His sword techniques were even better. They could fling slashes with unusual powers as well. Including the technique that saved Vivian from the life of being a slaved minion doing clawgirl evil.

Vivian murmured awake. "Romeo?"

"Vivian," he said and gave her a reassuring hug.

A hug she returned. Returned far too nervously.

"I just totally had a nightmare," she said, "Of the life I like, would have had to live, if ... you know."

Romeo hugged her snug again. "I know, and—"

The crow cawed loud and clear. All three eyes stared **hard** at Romeo.

Freezing him? His body ... it wouldn't move. Refused to move. Breathe even.

His sword ... he needed to reach his sword ...

But how?

"Romeo?' Vivian said, "Wha ... no, that crow!"

The crow cackled?! Romeo tried to grit his teeth, but no.

No movement.

Yet.

"Return to me, Vivian," the crow said, "and all will be forgiven."

Vivian gasped. Tightened her grip on Romeo.

"What?!" she said, "Never! I hate you! I—"

"What you think," the crow said, "doesn't matter. You, you and your kind exist to serve the Baelzog. Nothing more. Nothing less."

Romeo tried to snarl. But again. Nothing.

But Vivian hissed. Louder and angry serpent style.

"I'd rather die than—" Vivian said.

"Your death," the crow said, "is not yours to choose, clawgirl."

The crow, its third eye started to glow a crimson red. A glow that made Vivian tremble. Whimper terrified.

"No," Vivian said, "Not again ..."

And there was nothing Romeo could do—yet.

CHAPTER 2
ROMEO

No!

There had to be something Romeo could do. Anything.

His whole body chilled at the thought of losing Vivian again. Having to fight her again. Maybe even hurt her again. All to somehow save her. Again.

But Romeo was paralyzed. Somehow. Like a mouse caught in a serpent's gaze.

Except the gaze—from that sinister crow.

No. Pa taught him how to escape that kind of gaze. Long ago. Back when a giant python was stalking the village he used to live in. It was a giant monster of a snake that ate several sheep a night and almost ate Romeo too.

Except pain. Intense pain.

At the right moment.

So right now, don't focus on the grunts and growls of the

gigantic beasts below them. Or how sweaty hot it was. Or even his own racing heartbeat.

Forget how Vivian and her fine, fine ass was so tense yet still pressed so wonderfully soft against his crotch.

Pleasure was certain death right now.

Worse than death for Vivian.

At the end of this long twisted branch that Vivian and Romeo both sat together on, the big fat crow in the moonlight, the crimson glow of that crow's third eye, he'd only have him a few more moments, he was sure of that, and using those moments right—critical.

So focus on the raw rough bark against his back. Poking his back through his vest. Through his slacks. His thick reliable suede boots. Not on the lichen and moss softening the mild discomfort.

No.

Focus on how, underneath that wonderfully rosy scent of Vivian, there was the sharp jab of the forest's musty smell, and that jab stabbing right up his nose each and every breath.

Like Uncle Jethron always said, trust your nose, and rely on it.

Don't focus on the other craggy branches around them. They hid them from most of the larger creatures around. That they were alone in this tree except for the crow.

At least, for now.

The other clawgirls from yesterday were sleeping in their own tree around the clearing. Best not put everyone in the same spot. Just in case of attack.

But they had thought, since, of course, they were clawgirls, that they could let out a warning call if one of them was attacked. Their reptilian underscent should have deterred the worst creatures from attacking outright, but ...

Yesterday it didn't deter the horse-sized jaybirds known as jumping raptors from attacking one of them.

And now, this crow ...

The pain of losing Vivian, of any of the clawgirls he just freed yesterday ... like a stab to the heart.

And enough for him to bite his lip.

HARD.

But he refused to whimper. Even move.

And reveal he freed himself from the crow's paralyzing gaze.

Until he pinched Vivian's thightastic thigh.

Hard.

CHAPTER 3

ROMEO

The moment Vivian yelped, she tensed even tighter against his chest, his crotch, Romeo was so relieved he almost let down his guard.

Almost.

The rough bark in his back, he focused on that, on the ragged bark of the lumpy branch beneath him. How his slacks only softened it some. The moss and the lichen some more. The smell of the lichen and moss from the muggy heat, more jabs to keep him aware and moving, just like pa would have drilled into him.

The tree shook from another beast striking the crack by the ground, no, the stink of carnivore too—a smell Uncle One-Leg Jethron insisted was because carnivores used their stinkiness to mark their territory so trust his nose when he smelled it.

The loud wet sniffs halfway between this branch and the hard stone ground ...

The scrapping of thick razor claws against the stone ground ...

Leaving the tree—not an option.

Aunt Tilda would never forgive Romeo if he disappeared like his parents so long ago. As hard as she was on the girls she kept at Honey Heart Resort, since, of course, she paid their families good money to let them work there, to pleasure patrons with games and other entertainment that they'd never get the chance to earn so much, to maybe even marry into nobility, or other such rich men.

Sigh.

Good thing the pale moonlight revealed how much the crow suddenly flinched. Flinched so hard the thinning end of the branch bend down quick, hard, and creaked louder than the crow's own painful caw.

Pa would be proud.

Grandpa too.

Despite the bitter taste in his mouth for hurting Vivian. If she didn't understand, then she wasn't that right girl for him, yet ...

Vivian giggled. "Nice one Romeo."

And then elbowed his gut **hard**.

Good. She understood, but wasn't a pushover either.

As expected.

Vivian whipped out her pink scimitars. Snapped their pommels together into a wicked pink bow.

While Romeo still held her tight from behind.

"Time to eat steel, clawgirl style," Vivian said, and drew a pink steel bolt at the bird.

When the crow cawed panicked.

"Wait! Wait!" the crow said, "Kill me, and you'll never find the rest of your pack. Never!"

"My friends!" Vivian said, "What did you like, do to them!"

"You escaped, this time," the crow said, "but the others ..."

"Give them back!" Vivian said, and drew her bolt tighter, but didn't loose it.

Romeo didn't dare grab his harpe either.

Not yet.

"Fetch me," the crow said, "The Savage Sword of Shadow Forest—"

Romeo snarled this time. He'd heard of that blade. A blade that slew several dragotroll warlocks before somehow being lost centuries ago when a trio of dragotroll warlocks tried to summon a baelzog.

And, supposedly, it was a blade that would only humor a sword master to wield it. Only the right, worthy sword master—or else it would somehow kill those the wielder prized most.

Not a blade worth wielding, but ... it was a blade that would slice through anything. Kill anything.

Even a baelzog.

Or ... maybe, even, the seal on their prison.

"Fetch you some legendary blade?" he said, "Never! Even if we knew where it was—"

"Fine," the crow said, "Then your other pretty little claw-girls all die awfully slow and painfully. Such a waste. They could have been such wonderful honey horrors. With the right training. Whore training, that is."

Vivian elbowed Romeo in the gut again. Hard and painful.

Enough to break another paralysis before Romeo even realized he was getting paralyzed again.

Then she hissed. Very serpent reptilian. Enough to send a shiver up Romeo's spine. Vivian could very much go evil clawgirl but on monsters that deserved it.

"Don't hurt them," she said, "At all, and we'll like, get your stupid blade. Tell us where it is."

The crow chuckled. "It's not far. Vanessa will guide you."

"Vanessa?" Vivian said, "But she's—"

"Revived," the crow said, "Death shall not stop us. Your kind die only when we let them stay dead."

We?

Then the necromancer wasn't alone, and was controlling the bird directly then. Romeo knew that necromancer wasn't human. It was some kind of hobgobble, a legendary monster that warred against mankind in the past, and not so distant past.

Hobgobbles really were blue squid-like, (usually) human-sized monsters. They stunk strongly of rotting fish and they walked on land with its tentacles, but, in that necromancer's case, it was supposedly a kid-sized hobgobble that had latched itself to some poor fox and somehow enslaved it as a mount, at least according to Vivian.

But killing the bird wasn't an option.

Not yet.

Romeo huffed. "Death stopped that other hobgobble, what's his face, (after the right technique.)"

The hatred that radiated from the crow at that moment ... the deal might have been called off except ...

"Meet me," the crow said, "at the Cave of Coral Shadows. Or your pack of sisters ..."

A scream rang out--from a girl. Echoed from a far distance ahead of them.

"He-he," the crow said, "guess who just suffered for you insolence? You two know the rest. Come! Alone with only Vanessa! Or else!"

The crow flew off. "Serve in life or death, your choice ..."

Vivian hissed serpent furious again.

"As if," she said, "That necromancer would like, never give usss a real choice, but ... my pack sisters ..."

Romeo hugged her waist snug.

"We'll get everyone back," he said, "I promise."

"I know," Vivian said, "You saved us once. Time to totally save us again. With me like, as your heroine sidekick, thisss time, he-he."

And this time, Romeo pecked her soft peachy cheek.

Getting a content purr back.

CHAPTER 4
JULIET

Juliet knew she was dreaming—she just had to be—but the smell of peach pie was so familiar, so strong, yet so distant.

As if the strange red fog engulfing her was blocking the smell between her and the pie, and the craziest thing was that, as much as her stomach grumbled for the pie, she despised peach pies.

Especially Boss Tilda's peach pies.

Which it had to be. No one else made peach pies around here.

Juliet would rather sleep up in some craggy tree and eat the lichen-crusted gray bark for breakfast than eat on another of Boss Tilda's peach pies.

She could even feel lichen-crusted bark press, no, *grind* against her back and ass, as if she really was up in a tree somewhere.

(As if!)

Yet she heard, from a distant, snort and growls below her, as if giant beasts were passing by, sniffing their ugly noses and snouts her way but she was too far up to be their tasty little treat.

Their stinky predator breath even — ugh, almost as strong as those awful peach pies.

Since when were her dreams so ... real?

This was too much like her little kiddie days as a wild clawgirl. Before she was mistaken as a gorgeous but lost teenaged human girl and sent to Honey Heart Resort to please and entertain ugly but rich and powerful men.

Even the wailing crickets and frogs were weirdly familiar and way, way, waaaaay too close and and and ... wait, she was wearing a leotard? And thigh-high sandal boots? And even fingerless elbow gloves.

Not a nightgown. Like she normally did at night.

Oh nonono.

Yesterday ... Romeo discovering the truth about her, her being a clawgirl, and them, fucking each other, her in her reptilian clawgirl form too, and then the necromancer and those hobgobbles and her being slaved to fight against him and and and—no!

It was real.

Oh nononono.

Then ... she murmured awake. Even her head felt heavy. Her whole body might as well be some boulder. Her long sunny hair was covering her face until she brushed it aside. Including her now messy braids.

And ... yeah.

She was in some big craggy old tree. On some super thick high branch. Back to the lumpy trunk. Legs tucked into her stomach.

And all alone.

Because she now was part of a pack. A clawgirl pack. Sisters who all were once slaved by that same necromancer hobgobble. Who were all freed by her Romeo.

And clawgirl packs shared their mate, (or mates.) Always.

So gulp.

No fog though. Just lots and lots of spooky white moonlight everywhere. More than enough for her eyes to see even the big broad leaves.

See the hints of huge beasts below her that—nonono.

Don't look down.

Never look down. **Ever.**

She even had a thick belt on. With a pair of sheathed scimitars hanging off it. Her heart-shaped pouch with her life savings was long gone. All because that necromancer stole it and ... she hissed.

Yesssss. Hissed.

That necromancer was *so* dead. Romeo had insisted—no — *Juliet* herself had insisted, demanded that she and she alone kill that tentacled bitch.

And Juliet failed. Badly.

Getting herself captured. Slaved. Freed by Romeo, only for him to fall for Vivian, who was also captured and slaved, but could fight with blades nearly as well as Romeo himself, and ...

Juliet looked down. Stupid stupid stupid ...
And saw the unthinkable.

CHAPTER 5
ROMEO

Romeo savored the solid feel of rock ground beneath his feet again. Enough that he flexed his toes, snapping the sleep out of them. Loud and clear.

Despite the danger.

No telling what giant beasts would come running for a nice juicy meal of human boy and his sweet little clawgirl girlfriend.

But his ass still ached from sleeping on the rough bark of that thick tree branch. His slacks were a touch too moist, and all from the mossy lichen.

A fight to warm up. Shake the sleep from his body. Sounded good.

It was the type of thing his pa would do. His grandpa even more so. Time to take over that family tradition.

Despite what Aunt Tilda would say.

She wasn't here.

Vivian was. And Vivian was no wimp either.

And she was already holding his hand. Standing so close he could smell and savor her natural rosy fragrance. Some of her warmth.

The nightly cries of cricket and frogs and worse, almost enough to make him shutter, shiver at those shrill unearthly sounds, but compared to actual real hobgobbles, they were nothing.

The moonlight gave the ground a pale sickly tint, almost like a spooky pond of white, since the clearing was so wide and round. It was enough for him to see, but not see well. The trees beyond the clearing might as well be overgrown titan-sized bramble hemming them in, for all he could see.

Hopefully Vivian could see better. She probably could. That's a clawgirl thing, according to his beloved dime dreadfuls, and they had been right about clawgirl abilities.

Even how their archer garb could regenerate.

And how hobgobbles stank like rotting fish.

The supplies he was meant to bring back to Honey Heart Resort were high up in the tree. In his backpack, which, basically, was a big burlap bag with shoulder straps, but it should be safe and sound.

Hopefully at least until they returned.

A hiss rang out—and not from Vivian.

"Turn around ssslowly."

The bitterness in that girl's voice, worse than the unripe lemons Aunt Tilda used to stuff in his mouth for uttering the wrong kind of words.

As in words that hinted of fun adventure elsewhere. The dangerous kind.

Vivian even gasped?

"Vanessa?" Vivian said, "You're ... really like, alive!"

"No thanks to you!" Vanessa said. "Now turn around ssslowly. Hands away from your weapons."

"But ... I ..." Vivian said.

Romeo gave Vivian's hand a comforting squeeze.

"Okay," Romeo said, "Slow and—"

"Who ssssaid you could ssspeak, *boy?*" Vanessa said.

Yeah. Okay. Not unexpected.

He was the one who kind actually "killed" her yesterday. His magical crescent blade, the blade he knew as a harpe, well, he had sliced up through her gut and out of her chest. Slicing through her archer garb *and* scales easily.

Never mind moments before she had tried to ambush him. Using some kind of serpent-eye technique.

While blabbering on about slaughtering more men and boys.

As in she had not only killed, but enjoyed it. Hoped to keep on killing. Unlike Vivian and Juliet, and even all the others, who clearly were simply trying to make the best of their awful situation.

So Romeo only nodded. Careful not even to apologize, which would require speaking, and give Vanessa another excuse to abuse them.

Vanessa hissed again anyway. As fierce and angry as expected.

"Not even an apology," she said, "Now turn! Slowly!"

Romeo let go of Vivian's hand and turned slowly and steadily. Facing Vivian for a few moments. She was so wide-eyed and terrified, yet that wink of her eyes away from Vanessa, clearly, she was far from panicking. From freezing. His own heart was racing like crazy, and hers must of ben too.

But they both turned around, eventually.

Tall and terrifying as before, Vanessa glared her brown gaze down at both Romeo and Vivian, but especially Vivian, for some reason, not Romeo.

Vanessa was a haired brunette in green archer garb. The garb was, except for coloring, a lot like Vivian's, except her leotard and thigh sandals and elbow gloves were all solid bright green. It went well against her tanned dark skin, but there was no sign of the damage her inflicted through her chest.

No blood stains either.

And her quiver looked more than full, while her wicked scimitars were made of human bones, just like Vivian's, and were ready, held tight in her hands, and ready to slash them both dead at the slightest provocation.

Romeo dared not reach for his own blade.

Yet.

They both needed a guide and Vanessa, apparently, the only one available for now.

Vivian even raised her hands. As if surrendering.

Good idea.

Romeo did too.

Neither appeared to please Vanessa. At all.

"First some ground rules," Vanessa said, "No touching your weapons without my permission—or elsssse."

Vivian gulped. "If we're like, attacked?"

"Then *like*, die like me," Vanessa said, "and trust in *our* master to revive you."

"Or?" Vivian said.

"No or," Vanessa said, "Hope you don't die, Vivian, Death isn't that *like*, fun."

Romeo had to butt in. "I—"

Vanessa hissed furious at him.

"Do. NOT. speak. **boy**," Vanessa said, "But don't worry. Our master can revive you too. Sort of. With her spores. So living, almost as bad as dying but guys like you totally deserve it, right Vivian?

"No!" Vivian said, "He only—"

"Killed me," Vanessa said, "but let you live. All you others got to live while I got killed so painfully and horribly and you should have died too. Just as horribly and awfully."

"I ..." Vivian said, and gulped.

Nodded.

Clearly, she finally realized there was no way to win Vanessa over. They were enemies forced to work together. That was all.

"I'm alive," Vivian said, "and free. And I intend to stay that way."

But that wicked grin of Vanessa's spreading rapidly over her face, Romeo knew they were in deep trouble.

"But for how long?" Vanessa said.

Trouble that now, clearly, would be aimed at Vivian.

All because of him.

CHAPTER 6
JULIET

Juliet couldn't believe it. She had to be mistaken. But she was looking down, from all the way up this craggy stupid tree branch, her ass being poked raw by the lichen and bark, but nonono.

It couldn't be. No.

A wolf man?!

And the wolf man was as dark as the night itself. Big and muscular and bare in the icky fur. Its black claws comparable in size to her own talons, well, in her clawgirls form, but she was in her human form and planned to stay like that, for now.

But she never heard a thing about wolf men in those dime dreadfuls. Or from any of the patrons back at Honey Heart Resort, and some of those patrons paid the clawgirl bounties themselves, so they'd know.

Right?

Right, but Juliet had weapons. Her scimitars. Human bone scimitars but scimitars. Whose pommels could snap together easily and form a bow. Her quiver ... a quick pat, yes!

It was (mostly) full too. And her arrows could be enhanced, made more powerful charging them with her clawgirl power: lightning itself.

She even had the natural talent to know how to use them, sort of, apparently, as long as she didn't get too scared, or think too hard about it.

Gulp.

But her heart was already in her throat.

The wolf man was already by the wide jagged crack in the tree's thick trunk. She had hidden within that dark back when she dashed her yesterday. Hoping to hide, maybe even ambush Romeo, stupid her. The way she panicked.

Back just yesterday two jumping raptors—horse-sized blue jays that were as vicious as rapid wolves and all too common here in Shadow Forest—they both had attacked her. Hoping for an easy meal.

But Romeo had taken them down.

Their blood still stained, darken the rocks below. The gamey smell of their roasted meat still spiced the place. Even lingered in her throat. A meal like she hadn't had for ages.

A meal she made and yet also enjoyed.

Proudly.

Romeo had, rather than take her down, rather than collect the high bounty that would certainly be paid for an exotic clawgirl like her, he, in exchange for the bounty, wanted marriage instead, and wow, did they go at it like bunnies in a closet, he-he.

But all because she betrayed him ... because of that necromancer slaving her ... now Vivian ... nonono.

Focussss.

Her heart already jumped to her throat. She froze. Serpent still froze. Stiller than any mere human could manage.

And revealed that she was a clawgirls. Again.

Stupid stupid stupid ... no. She was a clawgirl now. Really now. Romeo had to be able to depend on her to fight. Defend herself properly.

No excuses.

So she stood up. Glared down.

No. Not just glared.

A serpent-eyed glare. The kind that should freeze lesser beings.

(At least according to all those dime dreadfuls she had to read.)

But the wolf only glared back up. its beady red eyes full of bloodlust. Its snout drooling stinky drool.

It leapt.

Grabbing the tree trunk. Shoving itself higher.

And higher.

Juliet gasped. "No ..."

Wait. She had to fight. Take it down *before* it got close.

No.

Closer.

She whipped out her scimitars. Easy peezy, right?

Snapped them together! Yay! She could do this!

Without thinking (too much) she grabbed an arrow and aimed at the wolf man. Right between its beady glaring eyes.

It snarled.

"Wait," it said, "I mean you no harm."

"Really?" Juliet said, "Then stay down there."

The wolf man ... actually let go of the tree. Waited down by the trunk's crack.

"There," it said, "Call me Jagger. You are ..."

Juliet gulped, honestly ... but a name for a name, right?

"Juliet," she said.

A loud wet and veeery deep sniff from the wolf man (Jagger?) below. (So icky it hurt.)

"That's so creepy," Juliet said, "Stop."

She tried not to cringe, but ... *cringe*.

"No," Jagger said, "My nose is my life. More than your eyes are to you."

"Oh, um," she said, "Okay. Then ..."

She gulped. Why did she taste wolf in her mouth?!

"I'll cut to the chase," Jagger said, "Your packmates are in danger. All but the boy and his bedmate have been captured by that necromancer hobgobble whose mate you defeated yesterday. Now the boy and his bedmate are being led to their doom."

"Huh?" Juliet said, "How could they all be captured?! Why wasn't I captured?"

"Isn't it obvious?" Jagger said.

Juliet growled. "No! Of course not!"

"Because," Jagger said, "you slept in the same tree as the boy."

"Then ..." she said.

Jagger chuckled. "Such naivety for a clawgirl."

Juliet growled even more, but made a point not to hiss. At all. Instead she grabbed the tree trunk with one hand. Tight. Hard. Crackle. Crackle.

"What do you want?" she said, and didn't hiss. At all.

"WATCH OUT!" Jagger said, "Above you!"

"Huh?" she said, and looked up and screamed.

CHAPTER 7
ROMEO

Romeo thought he heard a distant but familiar scream far ...behind them? Maybe.

Even if Romeo had already crouched.

Almost sprang into a run.

But it couldn't be — wasn't everyone else captured?

It could be another scream from those toads and owls, as Uncle Jethron taught him long ago, or worse, it really could be one of those legendary Screamer Horrors. A monster that ambushed heroic fools through imitating the scream of a girl in distress, but only at the right moment. What it looked like ... no one survived an encounter—yet.

Only tales of fools running off. Their own death cry and bloody remains ... well.

Romeo had to be strong. Save Vivian and her packmates. There was no chance that necromancer missed any of them.

That wouldn't make any sense. Who would that necromancer dare leave behind and risk further trouble to its plan?

Anyway, the oaks here were thick, tall, and craggier than Uncle Jethron's brawler nose and with them being so close together, their mossy beards in the moonlight scattered his sense of direction.

But Uncle Jethron did always say to trust your nose, but Romeo could only smell Vivian right ahead of him and her now-strong rosy fragrance. Not Vanessa. Not even the earthy musty smell of Shadow Forest.

Or any scent resembling its many dangerous beasts.

The trail they were marching on was thinner than any of the arrows in a clawgirl's quiver. Ferns and scrawny bushes slapped his legs like the crude patrons loved to slap the girl's legs back at Honey Heart Resort, where Aunt Tilda had him work odd jobs fixing things here and there and, occasionally, go sword master against Vivian, but only to lose to her, all in order to convince patrons Vivian was a worthy opponent so that when they won against her, their frail ego was boosted beyond recognition.

That for once Romeo and Vivian had to fight for real yesterday, and both survive the ordeal, it put a smile on his face, again. Made that rosy fragrance of Vivian even more wonderful. Using his technique to strip her beautifully naked, wow, did her cheek go blazing hot at the thought, again, and wow, did she handle it better than he imagined.

That she didn't kick his ass afterwards for it ... as much as he knew he deserved it, well, she admitted it was only because it also sliced away that awful slave bond away safe and soundly.

But he knew it was a once-in-a-lifetime technique.

And Vivian, as she admitted too also, would so develop a technique to embarrass him as badly now too.

Which, as odd as it sounded, was something Romeo that made his heart race faster, louder than any of the many cricket screaming its loud racket—

"ROMEOOOOOOOOOO!"

Romeo gasped. "Juliet?! I'm coming!"

And he dashed off. No hesitation.

Through fern and bush. Over fallen branch and log.

Right toward Juliet. Friend or girlfriend, didn't matter.

When Vivian cried out: "Romeo! Wait!"

But her voice, her cry was distant already.

His harpe was already out. Ready to strike the danger to Juliet down hard and quick. Vanessa be damned.

His nose. Trust his nose. The smell ... sniff, sniff.

Earthy moss and fern. Bestial stink. Somewhere.

No girlie anything?

Not even a hint of that strawberry scent Juliet always had.

Romeo stomped to a quick stop.

The breeze. It still cooled his face? It was coming toward him. he was downwind. So sniff, sniff. He should be able to smell Juliet, but no. More beast? Something like a cross between snake and bear?

His heart raced stupid now.

But the moonlight was his ally. His eyes, despite the murk, were still keen enough to make out plenty of the brush and trees clustered close together. Nothing on the ground would ambush him easily unless ...

The hackles on his neck shot up.

No crickets screaming? Or frogs or owls?

Just awful silence.

No. A predator was about to strike. Somehow. Somewhere.

And—

Vivian screamed: "Above you!"

CHAPTER 8
ROMEO

In that instant Romeo was almost already too late.

Almost.

But years of training with pa, of dashing, of leaping, and of ducking sharpened his sense, his reactions kicked in quicker than a viper strike. The blood of his dwarven grandpa, of powerful quick movements even pa struggled to dodge and counter, even quicker than diving hawk.

And that soft dark soil beneath his suede boots, good, the ferns and bushes in reach, even better.

Time to use a trick pa taught him too ... one pa used against Romeo time and time again.

He knew better than to looked up. He didn't even think to.

That was certain death.

But without consciously thinking of it, Romeo grabbed the ferns around him. Ripped them out of the ground. Flung them up. Roots, dirt, and all.

As he dove forward. Down to the ground.

And rolled away.

BOOM!

Behind him. The sound of a bulk smashing into the ground.

A bestial hissed groan.

Romeo jumped to his feet and wow!

Like a cross between an elongated bear and a furry viper. With massive retractable fangs like a viper. Massive powerful paws like a bear. Its stink, between a bear and a viper too.

But its eyes were closed, covered in dirt — but not for long.

Its struggle from its lunge had missed him. Its serpent-shaped head covered in dirt. In fern and brush.

Several pink sabers were embedded in its thick long body. Vivian's clawgirl power. To summon and command a bunch of pink sabers with only her mind and stamina.

So Romeo didn't hesitate.

Pa and grandpa trained him too well not to.

So with his harpe he sliced through the beast's eyes. Its hind and skull were so thick, he wasn't sure if he managed it, but the blood pouring out proved damage had been done.

Its yowl—more proof, and the moment he needed to retreat.

And retreat.

And retreat.

When the beast jerked itself back into the trees. Vanishing for the moment.

Vivian screamed: "Run! Get out of there!"

Another bestial scream above. Throughout the tree's canopy.

And this time, no pretense of it being a girl.

Running, Vivian was right—it was their best—no—***only*** option now.

CHAPTER 9
FLEUR

Fleur Killjoy couldn't help but shiver from the sudden chill in the steaming hot night of Shadow Forest. It should still be so hot her revealing leotard should feel too unrevealing, especially with her thigh boots and fingerless elbow gloves doubling as bracers, but her long golden hair covered more of her than her outfit.

Enough that Romeo shouldn't hate her too much now.

Maybe not kill her like he did Vanessa.

Even though Fleur was slaved once again to that awful hobgobble necromancer. After everything Romeo did to save her the last time. Did she deserve being saved again? No ... not again.

Back as a young clawgirl, she was more than skilled as a huntress. With her bare claws and talons, she slew not just grizzly bears, but their giant magical cousins known as grim bears. Yes. Grim bears. Bear whose slashes were enhanced by long invisible wind razors. Fur that deflected all but the sharpest magic.

All before she got injured in a fight against a trio of grim bears. Got mistaken for a wondering helpless beauty by a bunch of wretched bandits that abused her—but never raped her--but only because they could then sell her Boss Tilda for coin unlike most other slavers would pay.

And Boss Tilda knew better than to ask too many questions.

She treated Fleur well enough. Her sister Claudia too. Far better than any of her original masters.

But now the very spore within Fleur, within Claudia too, the spore from that necromancer hobgobble now made each and every breath of hers smell, and taste, like that awful rotting fish stink all hobgobbles loved far too much.

All Fleur could do now was lean hard against the thick mossy trunk of this crazy tall tree and gulp. She held up her pair of bright-blue human-bone scimitars. Snapped them together. By the ends of their pommels. So now they arced in the form of a wickedly gruesome bow. Her clawgirl power automatically strung the bow and let her fire rapid shots of icicle-enhanced arrows.

But the target ...

No resisting the urgency of those caws echoing through the murk. The necromancer familiared so many three-eyed crows that killing even a few wouldn't do much good. Her body was already eager to move beyond her own control. To follow more orders. Orders to all clawgirls hidden in their own spots.

Orders to ambush a pair of humans coming this way. Not that she could smell or hear the targets yet, but the crow said they were two men. Amazing brutish warriors who slew more clawgirls and hobgobbles than ... than ...

Gulp. Dying was guaranteed if she didn't try hard enough to kill then.

A painful and awful death.

Unless Romeo saved them all again, but the pinch squeezing her bright blue eyes, they had to be serpent-slitted now. Able to freeze weaker creatures than her—just like the legendary Velvet Ruins showed Fleur, back when they were worthy rivals and yet the best of friends too. Serpent eyes worked especially well on weaker humans, but others as well, as long as the surprise was genuine.

But probably not those warriors.

Not much.

Even Romeo didn't freeze too long.

Fleur pressed the back of her head against the moss. Took a deep calming breath—just like what her packmates drilled into her long, long ago. How breathing techniques were what made Fleur and Velvet the best of the best.

But now, her breath was anything but calm and skilled. Her heart pounded louder and rougher than any of the crickets or frogs or even shrieking owls.

But this kind of pointless, murderous fight was exactly what her kind was made to do. To thrive on. Yet why didn't she lust for it like Velvet did so long ago? Even Claudia, her sister, loved it. But Fleur, no, she just wanted to tremble, to run away, not ... hurt people she had no argument with.

Even if she had an argument ... no.

Don't be such a wimp. Velvet would slap her silly. And hard. Claudia tolerated it but only barely.

Fleur needed to return to being that cold-hearted bitch Romeo mistook her for. That he accidentally even admitted he thought her as. All because she was so ... terrified of showing him anything but cold-hearted distant anything. Her persona as the bloodthirstiest Killjoy.

A persona that even scared her boy-munching scary step-sister Veuve Noire.

And now that it might be too late for anything else.

Her evil monstrous breeding was the very reason she, and any clawgirl, could fire these human-bone bows without any real training, and fire them better than most well-trained humans could fire actual longbows, or even crossbows.

A chuckle rang out.

From the thin winding deer path.

A path that sliced through the ferns like a knife through the lemon cakes she so loved to have at that lemonade shop in town. The very shop Romeo also stopped by so often. Where she spied on him so much. His addiction to lemonade was almost as bad as her own. If only ... only ... no!

Focus on the fight now or else ...

Gulp.

Fleur slid down the moss. Crouching behind the thick ferns. Cover was critical in an ambush. Hopefully she wouldn't be seen too soon.

That she wouldn't have to fire the first shot. Back long ago she and Velvet competed for that honor but now ...

And her own rapid-fire ice-enhanced arrows …

A crack rang out. From a snapped twig.

Only a dozen paces behind her. A few paces to the side. Where the path came closest to her tree.

"Can you smell that, Docks?"

A gruff manly voice? From six feet of pure brawn.

"Yeah, Jeps," Docks said, "Stinks like clawgirl."

A deep masculine voice. From a guy with even more, even tougher brawn.

The ring of steel too.

Wait. Oh no. Maybe they smelled her? Unlike Vanessa, who somehow figured out how to completely hide her scent, Fleur smelled a like a mix of lemonade and lilies, and so many men at the resort liked that … that …

More caws.

More order.

No more hesitating.

Or else worse than death. Worse than … than … Fleur trembled. The memory of the agony of her last punishment— nonono.

A punishment her new packmates would share with her. Make her hated even more.

So Fleur gulped silent. No more warnings either.

Obey or else they'd all end up serving an even worse hobgobble. They existed to serve, for now.

Time to survive. As long as it took Romeo to find her again.

To … to … maybe …

"For Romeo!" Fleur cried out.

And leapt from her hiding spot.

Eyes shut.

Firing so many icicle-enhanced arrows the ferns were shredded as badly as her wits for being so stupid as to close her eyes and and and—

Gasps rang out.

Heavy breathing.

The smell of ... of ... gulp, that delicious iron bite of freshly flowing man blood. She ... yeah, focus on how feasting of the enemy humans would feel.

Both men were giant brutes. Towering brutes in leather loincloths? Their giant blades had shattered most of her arrows, but not all.

Not all by far. Plenty had pierced their near-bare bodies. Wounding them in nonvital spots.

Yet their expressions.

Not of pain, but of glee.

"Look at that, Jeps," Docks said, the one a pace closer to her. "Another one. And this one looks frightened."

Jeps chuckled so sadistically delighted Fleur had to cringe.

"Yeah, poor thing," Jeps, said, "Let's put it out of its misery once and for all."

Both charged at her.

So quick.

Quicker than she could fire.

Than she could dodge.

Could stumble back.

Could fall.

When thump thump thump!

The smell of burning man flesh. Roasted man flesh.

Enough to make them stumble to a stop.

Deflect the barrage of flame-enhanced arrows launched at them from their side. Another few dozen paces away.

But the smell of the flames, underneath it, ah!

The cherry must of her beloved sister Claudia!

"Leave my sister alone!" Claudia cried out.

Dock barked a laugh. "One for each of us."

"Exactly," Jeps said, "Now let's find out which kind of blade best fits between their legs."

Fleur slammed her legs together. The creep! Worse than any of the men at the resort.

Far worse. Even that creep that bought her virginity. The creep that died, was killed, before she lost it.

"My thoughts exactly!" Docks said, and let out a hideous roar.

And vanished. Tearing through the ferns.

Toward Claudia.

Her arrows rained down. Lit everything else around Docks—but not Docks. Who deflected every arrow near him.

While Jeps charged at Fleur.

Fleur didn't hesitate anymore.

She was as good as dead—but not Claudia.

Claudia who always looked after her. This time, it was Fleur's turn.

Fleur loosed all the arrows she could at Dock's back.

"Watch out!" Jeps cried out. "Behind you!"

Dock whirled around. Deflect all the arrows.

Just as Jeps did the same. Deflecting fire arrows that Fleur hadn't even noticed before.

"Damn bitches," Docks said, "Not bad. I'll enjoy deflowering them with steel."

Jep cackled like a—than gasped.

Collapsed?

"Jeps!" Dock cried out, and then collapsed himself.

Another chuckle rang out.

And a girl with a velvety voice said from well above, "Velvet Ruins was your deaths, boys."

CHAPTER 10
ROMEO

The moment Romeo heard that shrill inhuman screech from a distant, one so loud despite it being so far it shook his gut, froze all his bones to the deep marrow core.

The very leaves above him shivered like the frightened kittens Vivian loved to adopt every single week she went to town and collected more and more kitties until Aunt Tilda put her foot down and said ENOUGH!

(Never mind the cathouse jokes writing themselves.)

The very smell of the forest turned from earthy to bitter and fearful like the sunny-haired beauty Fleur only just yesterday trying to speak to him and stuttering like her mouth couldn't work right.

And Fleur, one of those clawgirls captured and needing rescue.

One of a few he needed to rescue. Need to humor that vile Vanessa and her necromancer master, for now.

His night vision was at least still as keen as one of Vivian's little kitties, so more than enough to make out the moss-bearded oaks everywhere and the fern-full brush up now to his waist.

Only paces away was the deep blooded crater of ripped ruined earth, roots, and ferns. It was right between him and Vivian. All from that monster which was a cross between an overgrown viper and a stretched-long bear. The one that attacked them only moments ago.

A monster now blinded—if only for the moment.

Now back up in the trees.

Readying for the next ambush. Screaming only moments ago.

Now far too silent.

Only thanks to Vivian did Romeo even survive that last attack. Next time her warning, her counterattack, would it be enough?

Better not linger here and find out.

Vivian was clearly eying the canopy. Looking around. Her violet eyes had gone ... serpent, yet strangely ... he didn't find that spooky.

Just as Romeo was about to dash over the crater, Vivian cried out.

"No!" she said, "Don't cross the crater! That burning smell — that thing like ... it's very poisonous."

Romeo nodded. His own nose only smelled blood and

earthy soil, but just because he didn't smell it didn't mean it wasn't there, as Uncle Jethron said time and time again. As a clawgirl Vivian had a far better sense of smell. And night vision. She just saved him again.

So he made a wide radius around that crater. No telling how far the poison whatever was thrown. No telling if his slacks and sandals would provide any protection.

But probably not.

Judging by the lack of eye-witnesses who survived its attack. Or else he would have heard more than rumors from patrons of girl-shrieks in Shadow Forest leading to disappearances.

Romeo gripped his harpe tight. Slipping through the fern brush. The quick rough rubs of the ferns' leaves. The quick snippy dings of their stems.

Enough to tense him further.

Up his caution.

But he dared not glance up. Not directly.

Not yet.

Only from the corner of his sight. Up into the dark murk. The mossy trunks. The dim moonlight splattered over the thick winding branches.

Branches some of which were now cracked and damaged.

Mostly ones above the crater.

No sign of another monstrosity in the trees.

Yet.

Just black splotches in the moonlight that could be tricks of the light, or other serpentine monsters.

Making matters worse, the ground here was so moist and loose underneath his sandals he curled his toes in anticipation of another leap. Another quick life-saving dodge.

Despite fearing slipping if he did so again.

Most important of all, he kept well clear of that crater.

The breeze ... so weak he couldn't tell where was upwind and where was downwind.

So, instead, he listened closely to the continued stark silence. The strongest evidence that the danger wasn't over yet. Just waiting for another chance to strike. End what it failed to last time.

Vivian rasping terrified — his own heart raced furious. Terrified. Of his own rasps of terror no better.

But no attack.

Yet.

Romeo reached Vivian. Finally.

Her own hands still gripped her twin scimitars of human bone just as tight as his own gripped his harpe. At least she hadn't gone with human bone for scimitars by her own choice. That decision was forced upon her by that slaving necromancer.

How and why that hobgobble horror of a necromancer had the garbs and weapons ready ... another question that would have to wait till later.

Another shrill inhuman scream in a distance ... of pain and fury.

Another battle elsewhere?

Or another trap?

Vivian met his gaze. Took a deep breath. Her rosy fragrance a relief, at least to him, and gave him another burst of strength to fight, to protect her.

"We need," she said, "to like, find Vanessa. She—ack!"

In an instant someone had grabbed Vivian's long pink hair from behind. Yanked her head back.

And pressed a bone scimitar blade against her throat.

Vanessa hissed furious. Yanked Vivian even harder.

"What did I say before?!" Vanessa said.

Vivian rasped. "But—"

"No butts," Vanessa said, "except ..."

Vivian yelped. Her hips jolting forward.

Wait—had Vanessa just kneed Vivian in her ass?

Romeo growled. "Vanessa! I—"

"Speak again," Vanessa said, "and Vivian dies here and *now*. I only need one of you. The other is a spare, and any spare that proves itself a liability ..."

Vivian whimpered. "Ok ok. We'll behave. Sorry sorry. Please. Stop. please ... ***ah!***"

Her hips jolted forward again.

And again.

And again.

Vanessa grinning so wicked sadistic ...

"Begging the undead for merssssy?" Vanessa said, "Pathetic. Where were you when I died? Oh. I know. Enjoying your little boyfriend here. Now let'sss return to the road. And if Romeo decidesss to disssobey me again ... ssslicing you up, so so ***sssssooooo*** fun I can't hardly wait!"

Vanessa finally looked up at Romeo.

"Now," she said, "come boy come, **bad** boy."

He nodded. Not daring to speak. Not risk Vivian being hurt even more.

But Vanessa needed to die again—and stay dead.

Once the time was right.

CHAPTER II
JULIET

J uliet was in the air, falling backwards, air gushing up behind her, whipping her air about, all before she knew it.

The superthick and lumpy branch she had been standing on ... where was it?!

Just thick musty wood stink. A stink that only a guy like Romeo could like. Like she was breathing wood and eating it too. Almost as bad as Boss Tilda's peach pies. Almost, but not quite.

Even with lots and lots of splinters.

Yet right above her—complete pitch-black darkness. Not a hint of white spooky moonlight anywhere. Not even a star here or there poking through the leaves.

At least she was still holding her scimitars, but not as a bow, but as two swords. She wasted an arrow too! How many arrows did she even have left?!

And the craggy thick tree trunk was racing up beside her. Up and up and up and up. Because, no, she was going down and down and down.

How much time until she hit the ground! She needed, needed to get herself upright, not falling on her ass!

But that darkness above her — that stunk of rotting death and garbage.

At least she was moving away from it. Sort of.

But not in a good way.

That innate clawgirl nonsense must be good for something. Please be this!

The tree trunk. Yes! Her sword. Just like some dime dreadful. She spun with all her might. Plunged the sword—no—**both** swords deep into the tree.

YANK!

Ack!

Her arms! They hurt **so** bad, but she stopped, hanging safe and ... the stink of wolf man ... oh nonononono. That Jagger wolf man was right beside her!

She gasped. At least ... she was near the ground now. Right next to it.

With heave and kick, she dug her thigh sandal boots into the tree trunk, but its mossy surface made her boots slip and slide and — ugh!

She yanked, but her swords were stuck!

"Um ..." Juliet said, looking at Jagger, who was right next to her now, "Thanks?"

Jagger snorted, or was that a sigh?

"Like I said," Jagger said, "I mean you no harm, but we are not out of danger yet."

"Ooo, yeah," Juliet said, "but ... my swords ..."

"Then I'll deal with this," Jagger said, "Please stay close by."

Juliet nodded, and looked up and ... barely managed not to scream.

CHAPTER 12
ROMEO

Romeo didn't know how long he was forced to march ahead of Vanessa as she held Vivian captive—that familiar rosy fragrance bitter with fear—but the endless quick slaps of ferns against his legs and waist, of dark loose soil filled with bumpy slick roots rearing to trip him the moment he grew the slightest bit careless, and countless bearded oaks forcing him to constantly turn and twist at Vanessa's hissed instructions ...

And his harpe sheathed. Not allowed to be drawn. Even if it cost his life.

Since it would cost Vivian hers ...

Least the screams of crickets and frogs had returned. Everywhere. As if surrounded by crazed patrons too slobbering drunk to sing coherently. The critters were hidden everywhere. As if even within the trees and ferns.

Except no sane patron would ever go out this deep into Shadow Forest, especially this late at night.

Aunt Tilda would be furious.

And terrified.

Romeo better survive. Aunt Tilda already lost her sister, his own ma. She couldn't handle losing her precious nephew too. A nephew she all too often said was like the son she never had.

Along with a bunch of her honey heart girls, even if all those "missing" girls were secretly clawgirls. Whether Aunt Tilda even realized it, Romeo wasn't too sure. Like ma, Aunt Tilda was a woman big in mind, body, and heart, so no telling if she did know and simply never let on.

It was bad enough that the supplies for the resort wouldn't get there tomorrow on time — unless Romeo truly hurried up.

But Vanessa clearly wasn't rushing. Not at all.

Every frightened whimper and stumble from Vivian, and she was only paces behind him, yet every one of her yelps was always followed by a satisfied hiss by the maniacal Vanessa.

When a caw erupted ahead of Romeo.

The three-eyed crow.

All three of its beady red eyes glared at him while it was perched in the center of a winding thick branch that twisted inches above his own head.

Vanessa hissed. "Ssstop!"

Romeo did. Hands up and ready for anything. Even if there wasn't much he could do without a blade. Pa and grandpa did teach him how to parry with his forearm.

As risky as it was with bare skin.

Going with this leather vest without any protective shirt, despite the crazy heat of the previous day, despite the muggy heat of the night now, definitely a mistake now.

"Boy," Vanessa said, "Kneel. Now!"

That yelp from Vivian—no!

Romeo dared not protest. He obeyed.

His hands now defenselessly laying on his knee, the dank soil soaking quickly through his slacks over his other knee, and the ferns now blocked most of his view of the crow.

A perfect setup to attack him. Kill him and possess his body.

Vanessa hissed again, dragging Vivian ahead of Romeo and right before the crow.

"Possess the boy," she said, "And—"

"No!" the crow said, "We need his sword skills. The Savage Sword may not humor a girl of any sort. Let alone a clawgirl easily slaved."

"Vivian here issss," Vanessa said, "better than the boy in every way."

"Yet she still suffered defeat at his hands," the crow said.

"Then ..." Vanessa said.

"She lives," the crow said, "only to control the boy more easily. Nothing more."

"Then pleasssssse," Vanessa said, "Bind her properly to our massster again. Holding a blade against her throat all the way there ..."

"Conscious blades," the crow said, "despise the slaved."

"But ..." Vanessa said.

"Silence!" the crow said, "Two wielders, not always better than one. He always wields a special blade. A second one may feel the ... desire to win him over. Vivian here has only the skill, but not the ..."

Vivian hissed, growled, but clearly didn't try to break free of Vanessa. Yet.

"Then like, try to like, ssslave me," Vivian said, "I'll totally break your hold myself this time and—"

"Silence!" the crow said, "Once I slave you again, you must never break free! No matter what. No. Your resistance has only dared grow. Like a cancer. No. We must—"

The crow cawed, flapped frantic.

"Enemies! Enemies!" the crow said, "We're under attack!"

CHAPTER 13
ROMEO

The bearded oaks around Romeo were silent. None of the crickets screamed or frogs chirped. No hoots or shrieks. Nothing. None of the racket that a forest free of local big and hungry predators should have.

But no sound of approaching enemies either. No cracks or patters from the ground. No crackles or spans from the canopy. Not even a flap in the air.

Yet.

A deep calming breath just like pa taught him, the thump of his heart, the music of battle-to-be, except for the chills racking his body, especially his spine. He was still stuck on his knee, kneeling, one knee against the soggy dark ground, his hands defenselessly on his other knee.

His weapon so close yet so far away.

The boulders jutting from the ground around him, they were dark blotches in the pale moonlight, but they were close by, only paces away. Their lopsided ridge was still too far to leap against, to use as cover against arrows or worse, even if the attack came from beyond them.

None of the trunks of the bearded oaks were close enough either.

But the smells, trust your nose, as Uncle Jethron would say, but Romeo could only scent Vivian and her terrified rosy aroma, and underneath that, even stronger, was festering filthy crow, from the three-eyed crow on the winding twisting branch mere inches from his head.

Those red gleaming eyes of the crow he dared not look to closely at, let alone directly at, unless ordered to, and only for Vivian's sake.

Thankfully there wasn't any stink of rotting fish, so no hobgobbles nearby, but in this darkness, he couldn't be too sure. Maybe more were around, but still too far away to help. This necromancer clearly wanted Romeo alive for now, and was clearly willing to sacrifice its own to accomplish whatever it was seeking.

That Vanessa didn't have a fruity clawgirl smell—did she hide it better than the other clawgirls?

Hide ... the dark boulders limited his view of the low ground around him. The twigs and the leaves on the ground, if whatever enemies were around were human-sized, even if they were four-footed, they'd have to crawl, or crouch, as they crept toward them. They'd struggle greatly not to step on any loud leaves or twigs. To make no sound.

Too much.

Unless ... he dared look up. Passed the three-eyed crow.

Its red gleaming eyes burning submission into his mind —or at least tried, but the pain from his knee digging into the ground, into the pebbles lodged into the muck, that broke him free.

Vanessa growled. "Romeo! Don't you dare! Stop moving! NOW! Or elssssse ..."

Romeo complied. For now. For Vivian's sake.

The crow cawed again. "Not the time. Enemies are here! We all must prepare for—"

"Who?!" Vanessa said, "I'll—ack!"

The sound of Vanessa stumbling forward. Thumping onto her knees. A pace to his side.

"Not ... again," Vanessa rasped," I refuse to die *again*."

An arrow had sprouted from Vanessa's back.

Then more pin cushioned it?

Vanessa slumped to the ground. Another thump, and the crow joined her on the ground.

Giggles game from the canopy. The creepy sinister kind, but given his company ... or dying company ...

"Romeo, oh Romeo, where are you going, little Romeo?"

A girl's voice? Lyrical too, in a romantically nasal way. So lyrical his head swam strangely, and too pleasantly too. Her voice was so familiar and yet ... not. His racing heart, no, not for battle. But that bitter tinge in his throat. No. Better answer. Somehow.

And cleverly.

Romeo gulped. His throat far too dry. Please don't croak.

"A little adventure," Romeo said, "with some troublesome

company. I ... well ... thanks for, well, feathering that crow and clawgirl."

More giggles. From several girls? In the trees?

"Only one? You still owe us for all zhat lovely lemonade."

Only one? Did that mean ... Vivian? Did they hurt Vivian? Wait.

"Lemonade ..." he croaked, his throat suddenly too dry to speak right.

Lots of girly laughter now. From several girls. The cruel kind laughter he suffered plenty from for years and years, but he dared not second guess these girls' nature or intent, especially after saving him from Vanessa and the three-eyed crow.

And the lemonade shop, he did, well, owe, well, a *lot* of coin for all those lemonades, and dime dreadfuls he bought, and well, the clerk girls were often plain but incredibly knowledgeable. Easily forgotten, unlike the Honey Heart girls from the resort. Well, compared to any Honey Heart girl. So easy to forget he ... well ... sigh.

They really were hard to remember, especially that the last one. They change so often that he lost track of them long ago.

Best not say that out loud, but the laughter was dying down now.

And no sound from Vivian either.

He knew better than to start a fight—yet. If they feathered Vivian, she'd need help, not revenge. Getting them to acknowledge a misunderstanding, and get help ...

"Name one of us, and vee'll let you go. Free of charge."

"And Vivian?" Romeo said.

"Ooo, Vivian. She has her own quest to complete now—if she wants to return with you, that is."

"You sound jealous," he said.

"Ooo. And if I am?"

Romeo ... wasn't sure how to answer that. His heart raced, but, his skill in actual flirting was ... limited, and Juliet had been clearly more into scorning him than friendly chit chat—until very recently, but—

A light thump came from behind him. And a light breeze.

One that smelled of lemons, *and* cobwebs?

Cobwebs, spider webs? Tales ... he heard tales of spider creatures near and far. Plenty of them in Shadow Forest, but any that would talk, especially in riddles ... and be so girly yet so sinister ... and clearly not a clawgirl going spooky either.

Time to gamble. Ma loathed a gambler but grandpa was a scoundrel of a gambler, and that rubbed off on pa too much, so both ma and Aunt Tilda refused to give Romeo the chance to get that gambling streak rubbed on him.

Until now.

"An archnofey," he said, "bonds with the man who speaks her true name."

"And vill eat any man who dares try speaking it and gets it wrong wrong wrong—he-he."

That voice ... getting closer and closer to his right ear, but no sound of a single footstep, or even a flap of a wing.

No other sound.

Yet. Other than his pounding heart.

But what she said, it was true, according to the legends,

but only if she's in her true form too, and she didn't tell him in that form, so ...

"You mean," he said, "feed him to your spider familiars."

"My babies, of course I do, but I do nibble on zee bones zhey leave behind. The marrow makes great yum!"

The thrill in her voice ... another chill down his spine.

"So Vivian is alright?" he said, but didn't dare move, yet. The silence of the forest was still deafening. The thump of his heart too loud and fast.

"Aaaaw, you care for that clawgirl. How sweet, no? Maybe she is. Maybe not."

In other words, stop blabbering on about that other girl, or else.

"That accent ..." Romeo said, "It's very much like Fleur's. You don't happen to be related?"

"Ooo. And if we are?"

That girly voice, right into his ear now, blowing cool and tingling warm and good. A lot like ... well ...

"And this game," Romeo said, "It's actually very much like that spooky game Fleur plays with her more adventurous patrons, back at the resort."

"Ooo. And if it is?"

Romeo gulped. "Fleur always said to call her Veuve Noire during those games, so ..."

"Ooo. And if she does?"

"So Fleur ..." Romeo said, "Or should I say Veuve Noire?"

A strong but gentle hug from behind, with a graceful sigh blowing into his ear.

"Ooo, I'd knew you'd guess right, my little Romeo."

CHAPTER 14
JULIET

Juliet stumbled backwards. Her sandal boots clonking the hard rock ground far far faaar too loud, but at least it was solid, beneath her feet solid, unlike that shaky branch she slept on.

She even reached for her sheathed scimitars, but no, they were buried deep in the tree above the crack.

She was completely unarmed.

Unless she went … went clawgirl. Reptilian form but the wolf man Jagger … he knew what she was. Her outfit was a dead giveaway.

But if he revealed the truth to the wrong people … no.

Whattodo … whattodo …

He said he didn't mean her any harm. For now. But even his wolfish stink sent zillions of shivers up her whole entire spine. Worse than any patron telling her their worse clawgirl horror story to her. The musty earthy stink of the clearing didn't help either. Or the reek of beast and rotting prey from high above her.

The lingering yummy smell of jumping raptor—no!

Focussss.

Yet she didn't dare look up again. Her heart raced too fast. If she looked up. At the terror still high in the tree top.

Nonononono.

Juliet growled silently. She was a clawgirl. Not some helpless little girl. She could fight. Defend herself. Back up this wolf man who ... well ...

A roar erupted from the tree tops.

A roar so loud her knees trembled so quick. Wobbling her so much ...

"Look up at your enemy," Jagger said, from beside her, "Now. Or die."

Juliet gulped, and looked up.

Again.

And screamed.

CHAPTER 15
ROMEO

For the next several moments, the patter-patter-patter of countless spider legs across stiff crumbling bark and loudly snapping twigs was the next sign of just how much danger Romeo had been in only moments ago.

Just a deeeeeep caaaalming breath, and the smell of endless spider was around him. Of cobwebs galore. Much like the forbidden attic back at home. Or the even more forbidden basement back at the Honey Heart Resort where Aunt Tilda kept the tokens of Romeo's parents, which included trinkets from their adventures that Aunt Tilda absolutely forbid Romeo from ever seeing again.

All to prevent him from getting "ideas".

The dark soggy soil soaked through his slacks and chilled his knee and shin, but no, Romeo refused to move yet. He was giving Fleur, or Veuve Noire the chance to make the next move.

Her warm soft hug from behind was reassuring, to say the least. As soft as a spider web and just as clinging.

But without the spooky touch.

He trusted that Veuve Noire hadn't harmed Vivian, but wherever Vivian was, she still might need his help, eventually, and jealousy among girls for the same guy … even if they all had agreed to share him in some kind of mutual mating thing …

And the bearded oaks around them were still silent. No hoots or shrieks or even chirps from crickets. No snorts or grunts from beasts nearby.

No stink of beast either.

The night's murk hid enough that countless spiders could have remained nearby and he wouldn't have noticed.

But more than a few spots here and there glowed a spooky red. In the shape of a globby skull.

Very much like a black widow.

Countless black widows.

Veuve Noire's beloved spiders, so no, Romeo shouldn't squirm at their presence, as much as they got his heart racing for the wrong reason.

But with Veuve Noire still hugging him from behind, her ample chest warming, squishing his shoulders beyond belief, and his cheeks flaring hotter than the sun itself, all Romeo could think of was to embrace the slim arms around him, and return the affectionate hug.

Veuve Noire moaned happy.

"If only we could stay like this forever," she said, "but we both have important things to do. And Vivian will not be happy losing her place to me."

"Vivian ..." Romeo said, and asked gently, "What happened to her?"

"You don't trust me?" Veuve Noire said, the pout in her voice very clear.

"You'd think I ask so nicely," Romeo said, "if I didn't trust you?"

Veuve Noire giggled pleased. "True ... true. Vivian ... my sister is dealing with her. She'll be alright, hopefully, but it's not us that will bring her harm."

Romeo gulped, but refused to growl. Not when it could be misunderstood.

"That necromancer hobgobble again?" Romeo said.

"Yes," Veuve Noire said, "And some of it will be up to Vivian to handle ... correctly."

Romeo nodded. "And our duties?"

"I'll bring you to our village," Veuve Noire said, "Only men accepted as mates may come, and even then ... there's precautions that must be taken. Please understand. It's not just me that you must gain the trust of to enter the village."

Romeo nodded. "I understand."

It wasn't just clawgirls that got hunted for bounties. Ever since that war against the baelzog ended so long ago. Archnofeys simply didn't show up often enough for most people to remember them as enemies of mankind. Even the dime dreadfuls didn't bring them up too often, claiming they were near extinction, or outright extinct and deservingly so.

"Ah," Veuve Noire said, "Good. Now let us begin."

CHAPTER 16

MACKER THE CRUEL

Macker the Cruel scented the delicious aroma of sweated fearful pig that wasn't pig, but something far better, a terrified pathetic human, and a male with just the right potential needed to release their true masters of this world, the Lords of Smoke and Flame, the Baelzog.

The warm wind gusted the human's scent from afar. A mere mile away, perhaps, but more than close enough for Macker to scent it, scent the fear and confusion, and foolish love toward an archnofey.

The wind itself shook the countless thick plumes of leaves, shook them like the countless frail humans would soon shake and shiver at their world ending before their very eyes.

The scent was clearly there.

Amidst the serpent stink of treacherous clawgirls. Clawgirls whose minds and talents had dulled, had become as weaken and flimsy as the bracken littering the ground of this forest.

Along with the stink of a wretched traitor of a dragon. And a wolf man. A rare specimen of his kind left. A race that should have been wiped out ever since they betrayed their true masters, the baelzog.

A fate clawgirls would soon face at this rate.

At least many of them would. A good number still remained loyal to their true masters.

A number who would be rewarded for their loyalty as well.

Deep in Shadow Forest countless thick dark vines known as the Strangled Deathlies grew up through the moss covering these thick craggy trees and hung off along the twisting winding branches. Many of their tendrils acted no different than spider webs, except instead of a spider trapping its prey, once triggered by a mere touch, more vines could come, attack and entangle the foolish prey.

Drag it into one of its many hidden mouths and digest the prey whole, slowly and painfully, savoring the prey's physical and emotional nutritions for weeks on end.

Just the thick rotting fish smell, more than a few hobgobbles had fallen prey to those many Strangled Deathlies, but they were only the weakest, most expendable hobgobbles.

A good reminder that even the lowest of the low should never lower their guard.

Not even for an instant.

Since the clawgirls who dared try defying their new superiors, the Grand Hobgobble Kings they used to command in order to control legions of hobgobbles, now it was those lowly treacherous clawgirls who would be tossed into those Strangled Deathlies as examples to all the others.

Their screams were more than human enough upon their slow agonizing deaths.

More than enough to whet the appetites for the screams of real human girls.

To breed and feast on them once their wretched menfolk were crushed.

But only a few examples could be safely made without actually weakening his own forces. Few other creatures nowadays could serve as such agile long-ranged fighters as well as clawgirls.

In fact, even with his own size, thrice as tall as the tallest clawgirl, and several times as wide, and all green-scaled brawn, the dragotroll known as General Commander Macker the Cruel surveyed his three of his seven captains.

The Grand Hobgobble King Trenchel was big for a hobgobble. Standing straight up, the dark blue squid creature, even without its thick dark armor, reached up to Macker's own knees, and its girth was wide and full of prey caught and crushed by his own tentacles.

Trenchel lurked in the background now. Savoring the chance to gain more clawgirls under his command.

Such as the stunningly delicious looking clawgirl before Macker right now. Her complexion was well-tanned, very much like the almonds he loved to crush and cover girl-flesh with.

It even matched her almond and vanilla stink.

She was slim and soft in the places she ought to be, while remaining fat and muscled in the tastiest places that even human males preferred such women to be. Had she been human, Macker would have saved her for a major feast, but no, she was all clawgirl, fortunately for her.

With long dark hair curled at the end by her shoulder blades, and a snug leotard of neon violet, with pink hearts in choice tasty places, that all matched her violet serpent eyes perfectly.

"Velvet Ruins," Macker said, "report."

"The archnofey village had been located," Velvet said, her voice still as velvety as her namesake, despite the delicious fear soaking her serpent scent, "but they still refuse to join usss."

Behind her move in two more clawgirls. A blonde as deliciously gorgeous as Velvet and spiced in even more fear, and a ruby-hair clawgirl, not quite as tasty looking as the other two, but close, very close.

"As I thought," Macker said, "and their defenses?"

"The Hanging City of Fangs," Velvet said, "I counted at least a dozen colored spider threads, each with their unique power. Thanks to the tendrils sacrifices."

Macker growled, fainting more annoyance than he really felt. Enough to make all three clawgirls visibly cringe.

Good.

They still knew proper fear.

"They exist to serve," Macker said "whether in life or death, just like you three. No need to thank them."

Velvet nodded, and clearly resisted the urge to gulp. The blonde made no attempt to hide that loud big gulp.

Nor did the redhead.

But all three tried to hide the tension in their bodies becoming far greater, but no hiding the scent of the fear growing deliciously greater and greater from all three of them.

"Of course," Velvet said, "and among the spider threads were spider creatures I didn't recognize. They ... smelled strange. Of ... sweet candies and—"

"I know of those creatures," Macker said, and taming them would be critical for later battles, but no need for Velvet to know such things—yet.

Or her two clawgirl minions.

Velvet simply nodded. Clearly too smart for her own good, but too many clawgirls were like that.

And why their loyalty was in question now.

"There were ... other things," Velvet said, "but even my vision couldn't perceive them well, but—"

"No butts," Macker said, as skilled as Velvet was, his own nose already had picked up the hints of what she saw—of strange ruins full of undeath and worse, "except your three foolishly fearful ones prostrating before your new superior, Grand Hobgobble King Trenchel."

For a moment her eyes widened in utter terror, but Velvet fell to her knees, and head touching the ground.

Her two clawgirl minions followed moments later.

Too many moments later.

Their silence ... not a protest from any of them. Good. Despite their shocked scent full of indignant horror.

Macker didn't like it. Not one bit.

But word of the other clawgirls, after they dared utter protests, that must have gotten around, even if they were healed afterwards, since replacing them took too long—for now.

Clearly, they had been made far too much like the human females they imitated.

"Grand Hobgobble King Trenchel," Macker said, "use all your forces to capture the human boy known as Romeo Bladell."

The blonde clawgirl her scent ... was hopeful? Good. The perfect bait.

Trenchel gurgled a pleased laugh.

"And the necromancer?" Trenchel said, "Her failure to retain those clawgirls cost us dearly. Even now, we still have two more to recover."

"True," Macker said, "but there was no treachery in her failure. The loss of her precious mate cost her dearly as well, and has inspired greater care and determination to succeed."

"Then the clawgirls who betrayed us ..." Trenchel said.

"Too valuable to kill outright," Macker said, "Use them well, and you'll soon understand."

No need to explain too much. Their lives would be needed later. At least some of them. As sacrifices.

Their screams would be delicious to the ears.

Trenchel wiggled his tentacles in obvious excitement over

this role reversal. How a mere hobgobble could now command the clawgirls he so despised.

"Even Velvet?" Trenchel said, "Her thoughts of betrayal ..."

"All too clear," Macker said, "they all stink of it. Keep them on a tight leash. All of them."

"As you wish," Trenchel said.

"Good," Macker said, "Aid the necromancer in any way you see fit. Get me the boy's blade, and you will also gain the reward the necromancer seeks for herself."

This time the hobgobble gurgled, and not just pleased, but as determined as well.

Perfect.

Now time for Macker to prepare for the next step of the invasion ... and the release of their true masters.

CHAPTER 17
ROMEO

Romeo woke up, and without even realizing he had fallen unconscious before. His eyes were still shut, then open, and yet ... there was darkness all around him?

Gulp.

He breathed in deeply, and ... ugh, it was so muggy—as muggy as a starved bandit—and yet it was thick with cobwebbed musk ... gulp, again, but no cobwebs in his mouth.

Yet.

Just dry sour fear.

How long had he been sleeping without realizing it? He couldn't remember any dreams, except the burn of endless flame and smoke and yet, no burns when he woke up.

So phew. It was just some kind of dream.

His back was soggy. A relief compared to the harsh burn

of his dreams. His whole body was soaking wet, as if Romeo had fallen into another hot spring while playing another villain vanquished by the gorgeous Vivian.

No pattering of droplets anywhere nearby either, but wow, another deep breath, and yeah, each and every breath was thick with steam.

Like he was being cooked slowly alive.

But what would do that? And not tie him up either. He ... feeling himself, and wait.

He was butt naked?

The ground ... around him was ... ah, soggy mud. Hot soggy mud.

Just like the mud pies in the jokes Uncle Jethron loved to make back when Romeo was a little kid. Using actual mud. The kind that perfectly resembled steaming gooey pudding but the actual mud was all that much grittier and yuckier. Pies ma eventually smacked both Romeo and Uncle Jethron over.

The very thought was enough to make Romeo hungry for some actual pudding pies made fresh and steaming by ma.

Even Aunt Tilda couldn't make pies nearly as well as ma but ... sigh.

Romeo sat up, slowly, feeling the darkness for any kind of ceiling or bumps.

Nothing.

Yet.

What was he doing before this? His memory was as black as his surroundings. He was sure it was important. Very important. Yet ... Romeo took another deep breath. No aches. No soreness.

Why would he ache? Why would he be sore? What ... what had he been doing before this?

How did he even get here?!

Rome tried to stand up, but his feet sank more and more. Deeper and deeper.

He tried kicking and ... oh, he moved?

Like he was swimming in mud.

No.

He *was* swimming in mud. Well, probably. He couldn't smell what this stuff was.

Bubbles popped in a distance. The sound echoed far and wide. Smacking against hard thick walls. Like Romeo was in some kind of dome.

Like that old rustic church ma used to love all of them attending.

But ... the sudden stink of planty decay? Like a compost heap. Full of rotting vegetables.

Romeo gulped, doing his best not to gag.

"Hello?" he said, and swam a touch faster.

And faster.

Just more hellos echoed all around. Confirming he as in some kind of dome. A big wide dome. Far bigger than any church Romeo could imagine, but the stink of planty decay was getting worse and worse.

Worse than any compost heap.

Trust your nose, Uncle Jethron always said, and there was no chance that stench was just from decaying vegetables.

Romeo choose a direction, and swam as fast as he could. Before he ended up a cooked treat for whatever lived in this muck.

Until a girl cried for help—a good bit behind him.

Romeo didn't think.

He turned around.

Swam as fast as he could. The mud squished and farted. Bubbled and belched. Stunk worse and worse.

When darkness suddenly overwhelmed him.

CHAPTER 18
ROMEO

Romeo awoke.

His back leaned and soaked against soft bumpy moss. His butt slumped sitting on a hard lump of a thick craggy root. And his legs were sprawled out and resting on soggy but solid soil.

Yet his mouth ... full of gooey cobwebs?

What just happened?

Ribbits and chirps rang out all around him. Crackles of unbreachable bramble shifting in gusts of hot muggy wind. Carrying the smell of fresh blackberries?

Romeo gulped. Mouthwatering. No.

Starting to water.

It was still too dry and sour. Sour from fear of that fever-dream of ... of ... what was it?

Sigh.

Just a dream. Probably.

(Hopefully.)

But in a world with real hobgobbles, and their evil magic, there was no telling whether even a dream could have real consequences.

But his stomach growled loud and fiercer than any claw-girl denied her ... her ... oops.

His newfound clawgirl girlfriends would *not* appreciate that analogy.

At all.

But his stomach growled for those blackberries almost as fiercely as his clawgirl girlfriends would at that analogy, and his stomach was more than eager to munch whatever black-berries he could struggle to collect.

It was still murkier than a clawgirl's ... wow, was it good none of his clawgirl girlfriends could hear his thoughts right now.

More like murkier than the future of that hobgobble necromancer that dared try to enslaved his clawgirls again.

Still ... hadn't Fleur ... no, Veuve Noire, only moments before, it seemed, she was hugging him from behind, and then ... then ... what happened?

His head yearned for a headache that wasn't. Strange.

As if that would be better than this ...

Whatever this was ...

He finally opened his eyes. Eyes crusty with unspeakable goo, but wiping the goo away wasn't helping? Not at all. It spread the goo to his hands.

He was still wearing slacks, that leather vest, with no

shirt underneath. He wasn't butt naked, at least, but why he'd think he'd be butt naked? Stranger and stranger.

Romeo almost moaned, but no, making a sound, a bad idea—unless he wanted to risk attracting ravenous monsters —so no. Not until he knew where he was. Shadow Forest, probably, but where in Shadow Forest?

The murk was thicker than ... than ... well, his own self at missing all the hints Fleur had left him and he utterly missed, or completely misread as coldhearted annoyance.

There were plenty of leaves scattered on the ground. All soft and damp. Easy ground to sneak up on someone like him.

A scream rang out.

A girl's scream? Just like last time. Back when a monster sought to trick him, lure him into its trap, or was this a genuine girl in genuine danger?

He still had his harpe blade. Strapped to his waist. The crescent blade could even slash through clawgirl scale, as he discovered against the vicious Vanessa, and very easily through hobgobble anything.

And his techniques, if he wielded them right, would let him keep some distance between him and whatever trouble was nearby.

Romeo climbed to his feet.

But his feet screamed in pain. Made him wobble.

Stumble.

Hand on his harpe, other hand grabbing the bearded oak, Romeo steadied himself. Peered into the murk. Heart thumping faster and faster.

Music for battle, but what kind of battle?

Another scream.

"Heeeeeelllllp!!!!" a girl cried out. "Pleeeeaaasssse! Some-one! Anyone!"

An evil laugh. "No one's here to hear you, serpent slut."

Ah. Not a trap.

Traps didn't use more than sudden girlie screams.

Something worse, much worse was happening.

Time for a rescue.

CHAPTER 19
ROMEO

Harpe drawn quietly but quickly, Romeo dashed for her. Mouth as sour and dry as the murk right now.

Dashing as silent as he could. The ribbits and hoots covering the quiet huffs of his breath.

The crinkles of the few leaves underneath his boots.

But batches of ferns blocked much of the way. Just like pa trained him, warned him plenty, he couldn't risk the sound of them slapping his slacks.

Luckily there was plenty of empty soil between the batches of ferns.

Good.

The ground, covered with leaves, but they were damp, and decayed.

Pa trained Romeo more than enough so that Romeo could avoid those leaves by instinct alone.

Another chuckle. A second troublemaker?

"Don't hog her to yourself, Gogs."

A shrill nasal voice as ugly as the words the man spoke.

"Now Tibs," Gogs said with a rough dark voice, "I caught the bitch. So I get first dips on her."

A wide circular wall of towering high bramble blocked the way forward. Bramble full of what looked like blackberries except they were several times too big and their color, not black, but dark pink.

Romeo gulped, mouthwatering. No time to feast on them —assuming they were even safe to eat.

Big if.

How many times did ma and pa slap him silly as a little kid whenever he tried random berries out in the woods? Plenty of times. And the few times they didn't, wow, did he end up regretting his curiosity.

Another scream. From the girl.

"Pleeeeeeeaaasssse!" the girl said, "HEEEEEELL-LLLLPPP!!!!"

That yell, enough to pinpoint her.

A dozen paces ahead of him. A pace to his side.

The two men chuckled evil. They were a dozen paces right ahead of Romeo.

Good.

But pa would never ambush two men out of the blue, not without being sure of the situation.

So Romeo swallowed his fear. Announced his presence.

"What are you doing?" he said, "Leave her alone!"

Both men laughed even more evil.

"What can you do?" Gogs said.

"Go away," Tibs said, "Or we slit the girl's throat when we're done."

Gogs grunted. "Ain't we killing her anyways?"

"He don't know that," Tibs said.

A whimper came from the girl.

"Please ..." she said.

Location of these men confirmed.

And the girl.

Time for the Slash-o-Boom Technique.

Embrace the silence within him. Embrace it as tight as his solid grip on his harpe. So taking a deep breath and listening to his heartbeat ...

Thump.

Thump.

Thump.

His heartbeat—a dance to doom.

To a slash that glowed bluer than any daytime sky.

It ripped through the bramble. Tearing through it. Creating a canyon. A wide path down dozens of paces.

Two sudden screams.

And two less men.

CHAPTER 20
VIVIAN

Vivian likey totallies woke up with a face full of cobwebs and musty spidery ick all up in her mouth and nose, and even over her eyes, forcing her to blink blink and likey blink. Her limbs were already tangled and glued sticky and icky in place, and so much so, even though they were spread out wide and achy, they refused to budge beyond a wiggle or two no matter how much she likey totallies tried to tug them.

This was waaaay to much like a damsel in distress game she had to play for patrons who were feeling totallies more adventurous than they ever really were in real life.

The kind that hired brutal mercenaries to hunt down a rumored clawgirl all for the huge nice bounty, and yet go all so cheapskate they'd fear the mercenaries would backstab them too, and blah blah blah.

It was even as dim as the basement she was stuck in during those awful silly games, except ... this place was more rocky, lumpy, and overall creepy. The rock was more dark gray than a thunderstorm and just as leaky, and worse, most of rocks were spires, going drip drip drip drip. Sharp and vicious spires, like a bunch of wicked spiraled sabers carved from the darkest of the gray stone. The only light came from the green orbs hanging off pale white stalks lingering between the spires and the walls and ceiling and they all seemed to blow in a breeze that Vivian didn't feel, likey at all.

It was all so spooky it pretty much hurt.

Water trinkled nearby, or echoed very nearby, but it sounded like the dankest and coldest kind of water. Like the caves she hid in as a little wormling. Caves that saved her life more than once from human and worse. But these clumps of gooey icky web were all around her. Rattling even spookier whenever she tried to move at all.

Too much like ... likey when ... a damsel in distress was caught by a spider monster in those creepy hero tales, but ... she had been walking, a hostage to Vanessa, only moments ago so ... huh?

When could a spider monster have taken her? And not Vanessa? Why? Why would it bother tossing Vivian alone like this in a web? Not wrapped in cocooned in a web, but spread out and all-too-free free?

Too totallies strange.

She could summon her sabers. Maybe. Thankfully she wasn't stripped naked either. Her pink leotard was snuggly on along with her gloves with arm guards, and thigh boots. Even her quiver was attached to her waist, along with her scimitars?

Wow.

Kinda underestimating her. Good but ... insulting too.

And sniff, sniff ... no yummy boy aroma nearby. Just the thought made her lick her lips, and cough at the icky cobweb around them.

So Romeo wasn't nearby.

Phew.

So going vicious clawgirl reptile ... her heart raced waaay too fast for a reptile girl, but letting him **ever** see her like that ... Juliet didn't mind, but she only did it by accident, anyway, and really, really lucked out not getting herself killed for that crazy nice bounty she'd no doubt get put on her eventually.

But ... what if Romeo didn't care for Vivian's reptile girl form?

What if he ... he ...

He ... as much as he totallies enjoyed her human form ... and Vivian enjoyed being around him, even if that smell got her heart racing for the wrong reasons, sometimes, she'd never munch him.

Or venom him up. As drippy as her fangs sometimes got.

Especially after that necromancer slaved her.

Could this be another trick of that necromancer? Vivian flexed her toes in her boots, and flexed her fingers in her gloves, ah, her body was still totallies under her own control, so totallies no worries—yet.

A click click click of high heels came, no, was totallies approaching? Weird. High heels? In this place?

And then that cherry musk, a familiar musk ...

"Claudia?" Vivian said, trying to lift her head, look at who was coming, not at the ceiling and its weird glowy stalk things and rock spires, but the web even kept her head in place, tight and snug, "You likey there? What's going on?"

No answer?

The high heel clicks came closer and closer. Spooky closer.

"Claudia?" Vivian said, "That's you, right?"

A sinister giggle? Enough to make Vivian cringe.

"Ooo. Who said I'm Claudia?"

So whoever that was, she was a dozen paces beyond her own feet.

"Your scent ..." Vivian said, "it's just totallies like Claudia's."

"Does this *look* like a clawgirl's nest?"

"No ... but ..." Vivian said, and gulped, "if you totallies wanted me dead, I would likey already be dead."

"Dead? Really? Then that **annoying** necromancer hobgobble would revive you and cause even more trouble."

"True ..." Vivian said, and gulped again. That icky cobwebbish taste, and that of spider ...

"And if you wanted out that badly, you would have swished your little pink sabers around and sliced through everything."

That newcomer, she was a few paces beyond the tips of Vivian's toes now, well within range of attack, but ...

"Unlesssss," Vivian said, "there's totallies a bottomless

pit below me. Anywaysss, I know ... likey how not all spider critters are ... bad."

"Bad? Just because we don't munch anything we can catch nowadays. Very judgmental for a clawgirl who'd be slaughtered by nearly any of her human companions if they knew the truth."

"Claudia," Vivian said, "it has to be you, Claudia. Totallies for realzie. What's likey going on? Do I totallies have to be in this web?"

A sigh?

"Think. You're not the airhead you pretend to be, right?"

"I ..." Vivian pouted. She ... well ... the airhead thing was a cutesy act, well, started as one, since human men were more ... generous toward a beautiful airhead and less suspicious.

"The spores," Vivian said, "you're worried the necromancer still has some control over me."

"Bingo!"

"And some spider mon...*creatures*—"

"Ooo. Stumble on the word *monsters*? Why the hesitation? We're **all** monster down here. Even you, little clawgirl."

"I ... yeah, we are," Vivian said, "and spider monsters, some, can mimic smells and sounds of their prey, and others but mimicking sight is far harder for us humanoid critters with keen eyesight, so ... since I can't see you, I can't be sure you're Claudia or a spider monster posing as Claudia."

"I knew you weren't the airhead you pretended to be."

"So ..." Vivian said, "how long must I stay like thisssss?"

"Patience, and maybe, I'll tell you later—he-he."

"Alright," Vivian said, "Jusssst ... let me know that Romeo

is alright ... when you can. Please, and my clawgirl nestmates ... if you know what happened to them."

"I do, I do, but patience. Later. Now sleep ... and when you wake ..."

"Let's have some fun," Vivian said, "likey rescuing ... Romeo ... to-gethhher ..."

CHAPTER 21
ROMEO

Harpe raised and still ready, Romeo didn't dash forward, no, he slipped carefully forward, careful not to step on a single twig or crinkle a single leaf.

No telling if those two men had allies nearby.

Or worse.

Romeo slipped right into the newly formed canyon splitting the circular wall of towering bramble. So many overgrown dark-pink blackberries had been obliterated by his Slash-o-Boom that a thick layer of their ruby goo covered the dark soil and shredded thorn vines for several feet into the bramble.

Enough that the incredibly sweet smell of the goo watered his mouth even more.

Beyond the bramble ferns clustered together even thicker.

As tall as his waist and not a single deer path sliced through them.

Only his Slash-o-Boom Technique left a path and the newly formed pathway was straight and a few paces wide. Leaving countless green stubs where ferns had been.

Green goo splattered continuously around too.

The smell was too much like a newly scythed field back at his old home, before his parents vanished and he had to go to the Honey Heart Resort and live with Aunt Tilda.

The path went straight into the murk ahead.

And the murk was so thick now, it was even hard to spot where the bearded oaks were.

But all those screams earlier were around a dozen paces away. Well within the dark murk. No telling what else heard all of that.

What would come for an easy meal.

The shredded remains of the two men would attract fearsome creatures too, soon enough. Whether the girl really was human, clawgirl, or something else, she'd need some calming down and then ... how much would she be willing to trust him?

A rescue was a rescue, but once things calmed down ...

No.

No time to hesitate. Later they could work things out.

Romeo upped his pace. His stride edged out a touch longer and longer, but he wasn't about to lower his guard, not yet.

No stink of rotten fish. Little chance of hobgobbles—yet.

Hopefully.

But given more clawgirls could be controlled by that necromancer hobgobble, and from a distance no less …

The stubs of the ferns pricked the bottoms of his suede boots, jabbed his feet almost as sharply as the many thorns scattered around.

A reminder of how much danger he really was in. Enough to send his heart racing faster and faster.

"Hello?" the girl called out. "Are you still there?"

Her voice was so beautifully smooth.

So velvety smooth.

Romeo gulped, upped his pace even more. His feet hurt from the pricks and jabs but the sour taste in his mouth … he mustn't get careless either.

That already cost him too much.

"Yeah, no worries," Romeo said, finally, "I'm headed over. Be right there."

"Um, okay," the girl said, "Please hurry."

Romeo nodded, even if the girl couldn't see him yet. Leaving her in suspense, no, she was right. Take too long, be too cautious and by the time he reached her, more trouble would come their way, in the form of nasty hungry beasts.

Luckily, no smells or snorts of wild beasts, at least yet. Only a few crickets and frogs screamed away. All loud enough to cover the snaps of his less careful stride.

Soon a gigantic bearded oak appeared out of the murk. A few paces to his side. Far enough that its base was hidden by clusters of ferns.

He hurried closer.

But that slight breeze into his face, warm and ... it carried a hint of almonds and vanilla?

With a weaker hint of serpent.

"You're a clawgirl?" Romeo said, as he reached what looked like a deer path that sliced straight through to the big bearded oak. He turned and ...

Oh. my. WOW.

One of the most gorgeous girls Romeo had the pleasure to lay eyes on was fallen, sitting sideways, on her knees, one side leaning towards the bearded oak. Her skin was tanned like toasted almonds and just as sweet but for the eyes.

Wow.

His heart thumped music of the foolish sort, but if she was slaved like his clawgirl girlfriends were ...

She was still six feet of curved sexy slim in the right spots, and heavy in the moneymaking chest spots. With big bright violet eyes wide open and lighting up a heart of a baby face framed with long lush black hair curled at the bottom, near her shoulder blades.

It was the kind of hair he'd dream of stroking.

Just the thought, more heart thumping music in his ears.

But despite his heart pounding stupid, her cherry-lipped grimace was clearly directed at his harpe.

No doubt she was aware of the danger it posed to her.

And her outfit ... ah, a clawgirl outfit.

Her leotard was as bright violet as her eyes and with pink hearts in choice places to emphasize her curves in all the right places. Even her thigh boots and braces were suggestively slim yet sturdy.

And no mistaking that wicked pair of violet scimitars. They were forged from human bone, like all clawgirl scimitars.

But these were already snapped together at the pommels. Forming a wicked bow.

And a magical violet bolt was already aimed at him.

At his pounding heart.

His harpe was too low to deflect it. Not from this range. A few paces away.

"Run now," the stunningly gorgeous clawgirl said, her velvet smooth voice as beautiful as the rest of her. "A life for a life, as little as mine is worth ..."

"Slaved to hobgobbles?" Romeo said, his heart skipping a beat.

Her eyes narrowed, but not in anger.

"Of course," she said, "All of us are, now. Their spore, I cannot resist it for much longer. Please. Run. Or I, Velvet Ruins, will be your death."

Just like Vivian, Juliet, and his other clawgirl girlfriends had almost been his death yesterday.

His thumping heart ... the perfect song for this lustful battle.

"Or so you think, Velvet," Romeo said, and leapt sideways, swinging up wide, "Puributcher!"

Wide eyed, the stunningly gorgeous Velvet gasped ever so slightly.

"So be it," she said, and loosed her bolt at him.

But the bolt shattered midair.

Loud and clear.

Just like her entire outfit an instant later.

Romeo, of course, shut his eyes just in time, and lowered his harpe.

"I didn't see anything," he said, raising his other hand palm out and helpless, "But now you're free of the spores. So Velvet ..."

Velvet sighed, but not unhappily sounding.

"Alright," she said, "You earned a look."

Wow, and her voice was so velvety smooth and welcoming, Romeo didn't hesitate this time either.

He opened his eyes, and Holy Mother of the Flame Moon, was she ... she ... bare utterly naked. A salted almond delight for the eyes and loins. Her stunningly gorgeous body was like ... like ... a warm drink of hot chocolate on a freezing cold night and endlessly more enlivening.

No.

Intoxicating. Like vodka-spiked hot chocolate on the coldest of winter days.

Except ... well ... that her scimitar bow still aimed a violet bolt at him.

At his foolishly pounding heart.

Yet her cherry-lipped smile reached those violet eyes.

"Just in casssse," she said, cocking her head ever so slightly, "you decided to go for more than a look."

Romeo smiled back, lowering his sword so that its tip touched the ground.

"No worries," he said, "I'll earn that too--once the time is right."

Her velvety sweet laugh.

"Maybe you will ..." she said, "and sooner than you think, my little Romeo."

CHAPTER 22
JULIET

Juliet screamed at the top of her lungs, and more. Enough to freeze utterly in place. Reptile freeze. So frozen yet so loud. Something she should never ever do.

Especially not around anyone not a clawgirl.

But up in that huge tall tree, up that crazy thick trunk, and right above that big winding branch she had been sleeping on before she fell and got her scimitars lodged in the trunk of the tree ...

A huge gigantic lizard with wings!

Wings like an icky, icky bat. Super icky, but far more scaly icky and waaaay too strong looking, and very very creepyish with all those pale white spines that could slice up anything that got too close. Its long thick tail was wrapped securely around the end of the winding branch like a python strangling another serpent.

A serpent that could soon be her too.

Just the thought … choking … no air … like now, her scream, too loud, so powerful, and she needed to breathe but couldn't. She had to scream.

Its big curled talons dug deep into the bark, sliced into the solid tree like it was merely paper. Like it was stabbing a flimsy book. Too much like her own talons against trees, or trying to hold a dime dreadful in clawgirl form, but that winged lizard made her own talons seem pathetic, and dull, and nearly powerless.

Even with her lightning power within them.

"Enough!" the winged lizard cried out, "You're giving us all headaches with that inane screaming!"

The winged lizard even had a deep growling voice. Snarled right down at her. Extended its long snaky neck down even further.

But didn't try eating her—yet.

But this winged lizard …called her stupid?!

Juliet yanked her scimitars out of the tree and snapped them together and aimed a lightning arrow right between its beady lizardy eyes.

"Don't call me stupid!" Juliet said.

More like screamed.

"I call them as I smell them," the winged lizard said, "and you, little dragonesssss, are behaving beyond stupid."

"Little *what*?" Juliet said, "I'm not stupid, I'm just …"

"Shocked stupid?" the winged lizard said, and laughed even more nasty. The kind that echoed everywhere in this dark awful murk. "Pathetic excuse. No wonder you choose that pathetic boy as a mate. Shared him with your packmates rather than—"

Juliet growled. Pulled back the magical string of her scimitar bow even more. Aiming that arrow right at the lizard. Full strength.

No chance it would miss.

"Sharing mates is a clawgirl thing, you jerk!" Juliet said.

"So this one," the winged lizard said, "finally shows a little fight—but only after a few insults."

Jagger the Wolf Man sighed behind her.

Only sighed?!

"Clawgirl," Jagger said, "If the two of you were deadly enemies, you would have been long dead."

Juliet growled, but ... damn it.

"So what?" she said, "I'm not dead."

"Not this time," Jaggar said, "but next time—"

"Next time I'll ... I'll ..." Juliet said.

The winged lizard chuckled. "Not freeze like a helpless rabbit? Not scream stupid like a dimwitted bunny girl?"

"*Fine*," Juliet said, "I won't, but ... *bunny girl*⁈!"

"No butts," the winged lizard said, "except yours being whipped."

"Whipped?" Juliet said, and the winged lizard uncoiling its tail ... "Don't you da—"

SNAP!

Her ass! The pain!

That tail whipped her ass! How dare—

SNAP!

She yelped. Gasped. The pain. Stars.

But she didn't drop her scimitar bow. Not really, but she barely held onto it. Her legs trembled so wobbly she could barely stand. Until she steadied herself with the bow, Using it like a walking staff. The way some hunched over and aching grandmother would use it.

"I'm not a kid," Juliet said, finally. More like squeaked. "I—"

SNAP!

Ow! Her ass! *Again!*

"STOP!" Juliet said, snarling, kinda, while whimpering too. "I'm not. Some bratty kid. Stop it. already."

"Ho-ho," the winged lizard said, its long neck lowering his ugly lizard down lower and lower, "You'll always be my little brat. Who do you think I am?"

"Huh?" Juliet said.

It even smirked at her. The murk didn't hide one bit of its scornful look at her.

"Figures," the winged lizard said, "Your nose must be truly broken. Maybe from all those fruity fumes you drown yourself in."

"My nose is just fine!" Juliet said, and so loudly her legs wobbled far too much.

She almost fell. Even leaning on the bow, not enough help. Her ass ached even worse. As if it got slapped again, but not snap, but but but ...

Jagger the Wolf Man chuckled, yes, chuckled. How that ... that *furball* dared to loom beside her, and how he dared chuckle, his chuckles were just as scornfully as that winged nasty lizard. A winged lizard that, that, that ...

A snort? Right in her face!

From the winged lizard no less!

And that stinky ... stinky ... wait ...

Juliet gasped. ***"DAD?!?!?!?!"***

CHAPTER 23
ROMEO

At Velvet speaking his name—a name he never gave her—Romeo gasped, jolted, and took a deeeeeep breath of the steaming hot night air.

And his nose ... only faint almonds and vanilla? With that hint of serpent girl musk that, come to think of it, he only smelled off of Juliet back when they were close enough, outright fucking each other's brains out, and she was in her reptilian clawgirl form.

Juliet who felt hurt about betraying him.

Despite it not really being her fault.

The smell of ferns shredded to vapor wasn't strong enough to hide any other scents, so little chance of a hobgobble ambush. Even the hints of the sweet smell of the dark pink blackberries at least dozen paces away weren't strong enough to hide that awful scent.

From the jolt, the sudden pain of the many pricks of the

ferns' stubs sticking out of the ground and into his suede boots was enough to prick him to his senses. The snaps cracked him back to his senses. His heartbeat music preparing for the coming danger.

But of what danger?

More clawgirls? Then why wasn't he feathered dead already?

The ferns on either side of him wouldn't hide anything but the smallest hobgobbles, and some smaller woodland creatures.

Nothing worrisome.

Well, except for Velvet standing her six bare naked feet in the stunningly gorgeous almond-sweet flesh and yet aiming her human-bone scimitar bow at his heart only paces away. That violet bolt matched her bright violet eyes ... whatever power it had ...

Yet she flicked her head. Her long lush black hair bounced as lovely as her hefty chest jiggled in the bare nipple naked, and woh, did she have some nice big cherry nipples on her incredibly large and ample breasts. Teardrop breasts of blissful joy.

Gulp.

The bearded oak behind her hadn't taken any damage from his Puributcher technique either.

Not a single strand of moss was gone.

Or even a bit of lichen.

Velvet simply smiled even more sultry sweet at him.

"No need to panic," she said, "You were my original target, but those men ... the bounty for my other form would have granted them riches for the rest of their lives, unlessss ..."

Her eyes narrowed a touch. And very suspicious.

"My clawgirl girlfriends," Romeo said, keeping his harpe down and his other hands very visible, very raised and palm forward, "would never approve of me even joking about snagging a bounty on another clawgirl."

"You think I'll join your pack of girlfriends," Velvet said.

"I hope so," Romeo said, "but it's your choice. No need to rush a decision. I intend to rescue them all. And I'd appreciate your help, but—"

Velvet laughed again. This time with a velvety happiness.

"Of course," she said, "To see my best rival Fleur Killjoy reduced to such a mousey wimp ... help me restore her confidence and her lust for battle, and I'll join your little clawgirl pack."

"Alright," Romeo said, "Just so you know, your clawgirl outfit will regenerate soon enough."

"I suspected as much," Velvet said, "but it's comforting to know I will not have to fight and adventure all in the nude, as much as you would enjoy it."

She even gave him a lush wink.

The thought ... oh no, Romeo, his cheeks, they went bonfire on him.

A bonfire that spread to his face.

And beyond.

"I ..." he said, "really would enjoy that."

Velvet laughed again? "Then maybe I'll do so anyway."

That ... "What? You will?"

"Distracting you is so fun," Velvet said, "and my future mate should prove able to resist my charm enough to fight alongside my nude self, of course."

Romeo gulped. "Of course."

And now, he trembled, full of the stupidest kind of excitement, and yet Velvet only looked happier at his reaction.

"Just like how," Velvet said, smiling even brighter, "my former allies have surrounded us. Time to see who lives and who dies, right my love?"

"Right ..." Romeo said, his heart stopping, "Wait, what?"

Velvet giggled, rolling her head even more excited than before.

"You hear me," she said, "Let's ssssee if you can save more clawgirls—or ssslay your former loves."

Now his heart leapt to his throat. The muggy air tickling his whole body. Sweat chilling him. Tickling him painfully. Too much like when pa ambushed Romeo with a clever question at the worst possible time.

One he better answer right or else no dinner.

Or in this case, no more clawgirl loves.

Maybe not even Velvet here.

"I'll rescue them all," Romeo said, heart racing even faster and faster now, "even you, if you get spored again. Just watch me and—"

"More than watch," Velvet said, "I'll fight alongside you— for now."

And without lowering her bow, or even changing its aim quite yet, she strutted right toward him. Her movement was as graceful as a slithering snake yet as stunningly gorgeous as

... as ... as any Honey Heart girl ever could be. Her almond and vanilla scent became even stronger as she came closer.

Outright intoxicating.

His thoughts, full of lusting stupid. Just the thought of her being so close ... so eager to become his lover.

Gulp. Despite that violet bolt aimed at him.

Double gulp.

Especially when Velvet swung around. Her warm breeze cooled him yet sent the rest of his body blazing with lust.

She pressed her slim naked back against his. If only he hadn't worn a vest either. She was so tall, he was so short compared to her, that the top of his head only reached the top of her back.

"They'll be here," Velvet said, and rolled her head back, on top of his own, and racing his heart even stupider, "any moment now. Be on guard. I'd hate to die with you. They'll force me to revive and serve even more bound to them."

"Just like Vanessa," Romeo said.

"You know Vanessa?" Velvet said, "She's quite the vicious one."

"I ... well ..." Romeo said.

"Oh," Velvet said, and took a loud deep sniff, "so you have killed a clawgirl."

"My first and only clawgirl kill," Romeo said, his heart sinking quicker and louder than a pebble in a river's rapids.

"Hopefully not your last," Velvet said, "not all of ussss deserve better. Luckily for you I don't hate handsome boys, even short ones like you. Plenty of my kind do. Even Fleur once did but now ... I suspect only her sister Claudia still carries some grudges, so be careful. Ah. They are here."

And the utter sudden silence ... Romeo nodded.

"Time to show them," he said, "what a good free clawgirl and her true love can do together."

Velvet laughed playfully happy.

"True love?" she said, "Let's ssssee about that."

So Romeo bopped his behind gently against her fine one.

Her gasp. Jolt. And playful huff.

"Looks like," Romeo said, "I'm not the only one getting distracted."

"Ooo," Velvet said, "to think you'd catch on so quickly ... maybe you are a true love after all."

"Maybe?" Romeo said.

But Velvet only laughed again.

"So quick," she said, "Show them your blade is even quicker!"

And that strong hint of rotting fish suddenly in the air ... Romeo lifted his harpe.

"Time for some calamari surprise," he said.

CHAPTER 24
ROMEO

And calamari surprise was right.

Romeo crouched ready now. The stubs of the shredded ferns stabbed thoroughly through the bottoms of his feet, as if his suede boots were no protection at all, but he still gripped the soil with his toes tightly.

The smell of shredded ferns, of that almonds and vanilla scent of that stunningly gorgeous Velvet Ruins—even with that hint of serpent girl musk—of earthy soil and sweet ruby goo mingled with blackberries from a distance.

All now being smothered by that awful rotting fish stink.

Hobgobbles.

Plenty crackles. Snaps. Slaps. From all around them.

From ferns being ruined.

But the dark murk hid the enemy all too well.

So far.

Around them the ferns came up to Romeo's waist. To

Velvet's hips. So the ferns were tall enough to hide shorter, weaker hobgobbles—if those squid creatures approached in a clever careful fashion.

But the noise suggested an all-out rushed attack.

Worse, from his Slash-o-Boom Technique before, the line of shredded ferns would give a large party of hobgobbles an easy way to come charging to them.

The bramble would only hem Romeo and Velvet in—if they had to run, and if they ran in the wrong direction.

But that wasn't it.

Glancing up, Romeo noted no branches were close enough to the ground. Good.

Little chance any hobgobbles would climb the bearded oaks and reach the lower branches, but if there were other clawgirls about ... no doubt they could leap between tree branches and shower down bolts from above.

Any moment now ...

A crackle from above. Somewhere in the murk. All around them.

And high above them.

The snaps of bark being stepping on.

"Velvet," Romeo said, "the clawgirls from above—"

"Leave them to me," Velvet said, "if it comes to that. Ssslaying your former loves must be hard."

"No, I'll save them," Romeo said, "With my Puributcher Technique."

"And what a perverted technique it is," Velvet said, but not unpleasantly.

Romeo chuckled. "As perverted as you, it seems."

"Let's ssssee about that," Velvet said.

Romeo tried to bop her fine behind again, but she bopped his instead.

He didn't yelp, but couldn't help but smile even more perverted.

Yet glance up one more time.

The murk was silent.

Too silent now.

"But those hobgobbles," he said, "they'll interfere. I can smell them but nothing else—yet."

"Oh, true, they're coming," Velvet said, "I can hear them as well. There's lots of them, my love, so be ready to throw some of those big flying slashes around. My bolts can only trim their numbers down so much. Especially if I must take down my former girlfriends at the same time."

Romeo peered into the murk even more. His night vision nowhere near good enough yet he raised his harpe.

Took a deeeeeeep caaaalm breath.

Listened to the battle music of his heart.

"Which direction?" Romeo said.

"Ooo," Velvet said, "First strike, I like ... attack around ..."

She grabbed his hand. Her soft warm touch was still amazingly firm, yet gentle.

"Here," she said, and pointed him at an angle toward the shredded ferns.

Steadily angling sideways.

To match a fast-moving party.

He pecked the back of her hand.

"Thanks," he said.

Attacking first, without warning … no, pa wouldn't approve. Not even here.

So Romeo shouted. "Hobgobbles! Turn back now! Or face your death!"

Gurgling laughter erupted all around them. A few dozen paces away. In a circle around them.

But the most were in the direction Velvet directed him,

Still directing him.

So letting her touch fill his head with the racing thumps of his heart, the pounding of musical battle in his ears, throughout his body.

Time his Slash-o-Boom Technique just right.

And slash.

Slash.

Slash.

Released three giant flying slashes.

Moments later. Countless inhuman screams. The stink of calamari and rotting fish even worse.

Hobgobbles shredded within the murk.

"Time to swing around, Velvet," Romeo said, "Ready?"

Velvet let out a delighted laugh, and swung them around for him.

Just the breeze of her wonderful almonds and vanilla scent, even with that hint of serpent musk, wow, it made his heart race even faster.

And faster.

As fast as they turned.

No. Faster.

The music of battle in his ears pounded even fiercer.

Quicker.

While the murk still hid the hobgobbles on this side, the squid monsters were no longer trying to be quiet. They gurgled snarls and curses in their harsh language. Revealing their location: within the canyon he made within the wall of towering bramble. With an increasing amount of hobgobbles spreading out beyond it.

No hesitating.

Timing his Slash-o-Boom Technique and ...

Slash.

Slash.

Slash.

Shredded ferns and bramble soon mixed with shredded hobgobble. Countless shredded hobgobbles.

Twangs rang out behind him. Velvet firing her bolts.

More screams rang out.

More dead hobgobbles.

Velvet bopped his behind with her own, again, and giggled so sultry sweet ...

"Now for the real battle to begin," she said.

"Real battle?" Romeo said, but managed not to gulp.

"Of course," Velvet said, "You think my former master would only send a few hobgobbles this way?"

"Good point," Romeo said, "We'll need to lure the claw-girls close in and surprise them."

Velvet laughed again. "Easier said than done, but my love, I'll do my best, so Puributcher ussss all."

And with a swoosh, she vanished?
Romeo gulped, and nodded.
"Yes," he said, "my love."

CHAPTER 25
FLEUR

Fleur cringed on top of the high winding branch. It was thick with moss and even thicker with thorny vines ready to grab and strangle her, feed on her flesh and agony, but she existed to serve that wretched hobgobble King Trenchel now, because of that dragotroll Macker the Cruel, and that hobgobble insisted she stand ready here.

The three-eyed crow on her shoulder cawed quietly. Its talons squeezed her slim shoulder tightly. Its red beady eyes all glowed bright and vicious, giving Fleur just enough light to see the writhing tendrils seeking to feed on her.

Its caws echoed softly throughout the thick craggy canopy. Grunts and snorts came from the ground below, but none from the branches around her.

As if the beasts of Shadow Forest knew better than to interfere.

Save Fleur with a less gruesome death.

The caws also let her know that Velvet's treachery was expected. Her actions planned for, and her ruin, soon to be worse than any clawgirl before her.

And a lesson.

Once that boy Romeo was dealt with. His blade retrieved and his corpse defiled beyond revival.

Below, there were incredibly high walls of bramble forming a maze full of ambush predators and worse traps. The bramble itself was full of large dark-pink berries whose sweet smell hid the deadly agony they'd inflict on anyone who dared touch too much of their goo.

Goo the hobgobbles below were now using to smother onto their many spears and blades.

Goo no clawgirl had earned the right to use—yet.

But all info the crow told Fleur.

Something called the Cave of Coral Shadows was somewhere within that maze. A cave with a key treasure needed to defeat humanity once and for all.

The screams of the hobgobble hordes dying in a distance. Killed instantly by one of Romeo's sword techniques.

Fleur only cringed more.

Soon she'd be at the receiving end. Of which technique though ...

Her heart raced faster than the other three-eyed crows cawing at each other. Filling the thinner branches and hidden among the leaves. Their glowing eyes revealed all the twisting and writhing tendrils hanging like skeletal curtains everywhere.

The tendrils known as Strangling Deadlies.

Vines that didn't dare touch any of the crows.

Not yet.

All the crows watched so frightfully diligently for more openings in the coming fight below. More routes to victory for that evil necromancer.

Routes Fleur once would lust to seek for herself, even if she hated the side she was forced to fight for.

Maybe ... maybe she should try ... try ... no.

Every single hobgobble below was revived by that necromancer. Granted some kind of immortality. Death would not stop them.

They would find that cave. No matter where it was hidden in that bramble maze.

But those hobgobbles could never live free of that necromancer either. Just like Vanessa was slaved, forever, until she somehow truly died forever, and Vanessa, standing at the end of this branch, now had two crows, one on each of her shoulders. She had her scimitar bow ready to rain death down on Romeo and Velvet.

Even Grand Hobgobble King Trenchel received immortality through the necromancer hobgobble.

But the necromancer was nowhere to be seen. Keeping herself far and save from the dangers of the maze.

From Romeo himself.

Cowardice that soured the coming battle. Fleur, her heart raced for something., enough to make her tremble.

Fighting Velvet ... how long had it been. And if Romeo liked that kind of clawgirl more than Fleur and her ... pathetically timid ways, maybe ... maybe ... he really didn't hate Vivian for trying to kill him. For going all out.

No.

He fell harder for her. As hard as the branch beneath her now. The two were excited to fight without Boss Tilda restraining them. Like how the tendrils were coiled and restrained several jumping raptors—predatory birds that resembled horse-sized blue jays.

Yet ... wait. The jumping raptors were silent. Tense. They ... they weren't being killed? Not being feasted on?

Strange.

Unless ... the necromancer could control the Strangling Deadlies too?

The odds ... no chance Romeo and Velvet could fend off all of this yet ...

Maybe ... maybe Romeo would like to see how Fleur could handle herself.

How well she could fight too.

Be ... ravishing and forward and determined and and and ... gulp.

A real menace to mankind.

Even if, deep down, she didn't want to.

Let Romeo see how Fleur wasn't some useless timid pushover like everything thought she was. Maybe ... embrace that cold-hearted persona and warm it up with stoic silliness.

Just like how Vivian was so cutesy sexy toward her opponents and they loved it.

Usually.

If Fleur was going to fight, to die for this wretched stupid war, least she could fight without too much regret. Make her death worth something to Romeo.

Fleur snapped the pommels of her lightning-blue scimitars together.

Gulp.

Prepared to rapid-fire countless icicles.

Whether at Romeo—or at Velvet.

Ruin their little romantic getaway.

Yeah. It was time for Fleur to embrace her dark side again. Savor the hunt. Even if it was for a boy she truly wanted to love, but … tragic love was the most bittersweet and wonderful, right?

Fleur … even managed to smile.

"Claudia?" Fleur said, "Let's do our best to kill Romeo, no?"

Claudia tsked. She was behind Fleur?

"By time you said that," Claudia said, and pressed her back against Fleur's.

"Zhat's vhat he'd want, no?" Fleur said.

"A real fight," Claudia said, "Like he did against Vivian. As long as we don't go as far as Vanessa, right?"

"Right," Fleur said, her heart pounding harder, yet lighter, "Savor zee hunt, but do not savor zee kill."

"Not too much," Claudia said, "but savoring it some should give us that edge Romeo enjoys when he fights usss."

"Vee cannot let his Puributcher technique touch us," Fleur said, all too aware of the crow squeezing her shoulder even tighter, "Yet if it does not …"

"I know what you mean," Claudia said, "What a creepy

perverted technique he came up with. I'm surprised Vivian was so lenient about him using it against her—"

A flash of violet?

Bang!

A bolt smashed into the trunk a few paces away.

The velvety voice of Velvet rang out above them. Hidden by the murk and some twisting and even more tendrils branches.

"Lucky for you two," Velvet said, "Romeo intends to save you as well."

All the crows cawed viciously at Velvet.

Fleur gulped, yet smiled too. Her heart racing so fast … rabbit fast—no, hawk diving fast. She was the predator. A clawgirl. Powerful and skilled.

Not helpless prey.

"You vill regret zhat," Fleur said, and smiled wicked sinister, as if the chance to slay Velvet turned her own blood to sugar—not ice.

Yet Velvet laughed even more.

"Has the old Fleur come back?" Velvet said, "Then come. Let's see if our old friendship still holds true."

Fleur laughed back. And not too strained either. Her veins seemed to be pumping sugar.

As sweet as the lemonade Romeo was addicted to.

All at the thought of a real fight.

Against Velvet of all opponents.

"Killing a friend," Fleur said, "is such sweet sorrow, no?"

"Don't get ahead of yourself, Fleur," Velvet said, "You're still out of practice."

"And you, Velvet," Fleur said, "are out of time. Claudia, I leave Romeo to you."

Claudia chuckled, straightening her back against Fleur's.

"As you wish, sis," Claudia said, "His death shall be quick and grand."

"Good," Fleur said, "And zee first to defeat their enemy gets extra boy flesh, no?"

Claudia sighed. "Never thought you'd finally say something so sensible. Now take down Velvet. It's time Romeo died once and for all."

Yet Fleur, it wasn't just her icicle-enhanced arrows that felt all too cold at their task ahead.

Even if the very thought also pumped sugar through her veins.

And the caws around her, not quite as vicious.

CHAPTER 26
ROMEO

For a few more moments, Romeo savored the lingering almonds and vanilla aroma with that hint of serpent girl Velvet left behind. His heart raced, pounding too loudly to hear anything approach—yet.

And too fast for him to fight to it.

Pa always warned him not to let his heart race too fast. The best counter was to find something else to focus on. A regular noise. A regular something else.

But the crickets and frogs hadn't returned to their chirps and screams. Nothing else he could focus his listening to. Not even his own breath. Deep and calming, but not really. His thoughts of Velvet raced his heart and loins too much. It wasn't just the hot night air making him sweat.

The ferns around him rustled from the breeze. A warm but harsh breeze. Tickling him. The ferns forced him to take another deep breath, and focus on their rustling.

Not on the fading rotting fish stink.

A stink that shouldn't be fading so quickly. Not with so many dead hobgobbles so close by.

Unless … they were had been reborn, revived by that necromancer hobgobble.

Romeo raised his harpe, ready for the next fight, but he could only use his sword technique so many times before he exhausted himself.

And he wasn't about to gamble who'd would get exhausted first—him or the necromancer.

He was sweating so much, no doubt Velvet could find him easily if he moved, (as gross as they sounded,) but where to go? The paths his latest Slash-o-Boom Techniques? No telling if they'd lead anywhere useful.

Climb the bearded oak?

The moss along the trunk was far too slippery. The trunk far too wide to hug securely. And the nearest branch far too high. Far more than several paces above his own head.

But no need to expose his back now.

Romeo repositioned himself so that his back was against the bearded oak. Crouching, he had his harpe ready for reaping horror onto his enemies.

Once they came, that was.

But his heart still raced too stupid for words at the thought of the stunningly gorgeous Velvet fighting bare utterly naked for him in all her almond-tanned-sweet glory.

A grunt rang out from the ferns ahead of him. Beyond the paces wide path of shredded ferns.

Then a growl.

From the murk emerged a gigantic bear. Fur as black as the night itself. A flat head as big as Romeo's own chest, and a snout big enough with fangs sharp enough to bite far more than just his head off in one bite.

Its claws were several times bigger, more curved than any bear he'd ever heard of.

Except ... it had a tail similar in to a mountain lion?

It stood on his hindlegs.

And towered so high above Romeo that the murk hid its head, and most of its chest.

It ROOOOOOAAARRRRREED!!!!

So loud it flung Romeo backwards.

Slammed him high into the bearded oak.

And he slid back down to the ground. Legs trembling. Barely able to stand.

But stand he must.

Or else no one would save the clawgirls enslaved by that necromancer hobgobble. They'd be forced to fight against humanity until they were no longer useful.

Romeo gritted his teeth.

Crouched again.

His heart ... heart ... that thumping ... was gone? His ears ... too silent?

No battle music for his Slash-o-Boom Technique.

Forget his Puributcher Technique. This creature wasn't slaved. Even if it wasn't it wouldn't spare him even if he freed it.

But those ferns by its hind paws. They were slashed well beyond those black claws.

Same for where those front paws had been.

Which meant ... his heart sank like a pebble in rapids.

A grim bear.

Its claws automatically used a wind technique to extend its reach by an invisible but deadly amount.

Romeo gulped, crouched ready.

"Come on little cub," he said.

Because Pa taught him more than one technique. Most required hearing his heart beat to the music of battle, but not all. Right now, against this grim bear, a counterattack should work best, since no matter the power, the counterattack would reverse the attack.

Counter Kill Reversal Technique.

But it would only work if he timed it perfectly.

Utterly, utterly perfectly.

And against pa and his very visible blade, Romeo only succeeded three times out of countless many.

CHAPTER 27

MACKER THE CRUEL

Carried less than a mile on the wind, Macker scented more than just pig that was more savory than any pig, more than just human. Taking another long sniff, underneath the filthy bracken and disgustingly mossy trees, he scented a mix of pig bred with beast, of bears, tigers, and foxes.

Of demihuman slime.

Even rabbitmen and their perpetual stink of wretched fear, especially their awfully fearful women, except that fear did spice those busty yet crunchy thin females even tastier whenever they failed their masters too badly.

This short-walled maze of bramble should filter out the weakest of them. The dark-pink berries would lure the dumbest of them to their foolish agonizing deaths. And the ambush predators would trim down the unluckier specimens among them, and luck was key to victory.

Luck and planning.

But no one could out luck some of those rabbit demigirls. The death cries of their brethren, of bears, tigers, and foxes— none were of rabbit girls.

Older women—yes.

Men of any age—yes.

Even their younger spawn—yes.

But their fresh young adult girls—no.

Just like none of death cries from traps came from foxes.

None of the death cries from fights came from tigers or bears.

Good.

Those who died here were not worthy of life. They would be revived as more of that necromancer's undead fodder.

The demihuman slime hadn't grown weaker since their wretched defeat in the last war. Using the baelzog's blessed magic to breed those inferior humans, and the last of the flimsy but tasty elves, with stronger bestial counterparts, creating weaker but more controllable beast men ... his greatest of his greatest grandfathers, Mackest the Cruelest, had claimed that this demihuman slime would prove more useful than those frivolous clawgirls—and in time, maybe very soon, maybe, history would prove him true.

As long as he didn't grow careless.

Too excited over the future victory.

And why he stood beside the one and only true and nondiscreet exit of this long deadly bramble maze. A simple arch of darkness. Dark from its angle from the side-path it came from, the angle completely hid it from obvious view.

But that wasn't enough.

Dashing footsteps. A few of them.

All echoing through the exit.

So Macker heaved his hefty double-bladed axe of crimson steel over his broad shoulder. It was molded like the skeletal death it would deal to his enemies, and more than worthy of the techniques a worthy dragotroll could wield with it.

Pointy orange cat ears popped out first.

And Macker swung his axe.

Silent.

Deadly.

Quicker than any beastmen could come.

Could dodge.

"I made—ack!"

One less foolish beastmen.

No. Three less.

And a tasty meal for those who—

A flash of sky-ugly-blue?

No. Sky-blue hair.

And azure rabbit ears.

Attached to a young, slim, but busty rabbit girl dashing blurringly fast, and yet that youthful rabbit girl musk, aaaah, even this girl was tastier than Velvet Ruins.

Even if her outfit was pathetic, it also was more alluring. Not a hint of brigandine, no, but that sheen, good, and that translucency, yes, the fabric was woven from high-quality archnofey silk, so strong enough to deflect most human blades.

Yet the stupid rabbit had her outfit consist only of a bikini top and bikini skirt. Both were dyed a ridiculously bright feather-me sky-blue and worse ... both were buttoned up with heart-shaped(?!) skulls. The silk was just translucent enough to hint plenty at her dark-blue bra and panties.

While her shin boots were as dark blue, laced with *more* heart-shaped skulls, and lined with fur similar to her own azure bunny tail's fur.

Yet, from the stupid shortness of her miniskirt, a hint of panties was more than visible ... fool of a fool.

As if any enemy male would truly hold back if they lusted for her.

And few men wouldn't.

They'd seek to rape her as well. A rape she clearly needed but since she was the first to complete the maze, to survive, she earned a reward, not a punishment, so he'd leave that part of her training to someone else.

For now.

She popped up, an oversized battle hammer in her arms? Its head was even molded after a pathetically cutesy and oversized skull.

"Azura Skyward ready for battle, sir!" she said, and hopped up standing in full straight attention.

Macker held back a grumble. This Azura clearly had superior luck for her kind, which already had superior luck to all other creatures, and the smell of recent kills came from her hammer, so clearly she didn't just run through the maze, she was battle-hardened enough to survive the battles within it.

More footsteps came echoing through the exit.

"Wait there," Macker said, and heaved his axe back up.

A bearman dashed through.

"I made it!" he said, "I—wha—AAAAAAHHHH!"

The fool tried to dodge the undodgable and suffered more for it. Bear stew sounded good, but others would come soon.

More failures to come.

Leaving only a handful of successes-to-be.

Like this fool of a rabbit girl. Even with the sour smell of fear drenching her deliciously now. Spicing her up enough to munch—but he had a better use for her. A use she earned.

She proved herself worthy of a true trial mission.

"Velvet Ruins," he said, and the rabbit suddenly stunk sour of extreme jealousy—good. "betrayed our cause for some human boy. The boy she was meant to hunt down and kill. Retrieve his sword for me, but leave the boy alive—for now."

Azura nodded. "M-may ... may I kill Velvet?"

Macker actually chuckled. A cocky one this rabbit was. Good. As long as this rabbit didn't foolishly steal the kill the necromancer hobgobble needed for later.

"Feast on her," Macker said, "if you wish, but kill the boy at your own peril."

Azura gulped. "Yes, sir!"

More footsteps echoed through the exit. That smell, no mistaking the vixen among them, and the fox men lusting far too much for her.

"Now go, Azura Skyward," Macker said, and once again heaved his axe up, once again ready to determined who was worthy of serving him alive.

CHAPTER 28
ROMEO

With the murky forest being far too quiet, Romeo crouched as best he could, legs wobbling and ears no doubt broken quiet, but the sour taste in his dry mouth, his taste was still working, but he only tasted awful filthy bear right now.

That and moss.

Since the bearded oak was behind him, as if the wide thick tree was guarding his back.

But it wasn't his back that needed guarding.

A dozen paces ahead of him, beyond the waist-high ferns and beyond the straight shredded pathways, was the gigantic grim bear. Standing on its hindlegs. Its head and half its chest were lost in the murk above.

An enemy worthy of pa himself.

More than worthy.

Time to prove pa's training sank in more secure than Juliet securing her little horde of coin in her pouch.

Well, before she lost it to that necromancer.

To feel his own heartbeat, not listen to it. The thump-thump-thump in his chest. Racing fast, but not too fast to focus on each and every pound-pound-pound through his leather vest.

Just like pa taught him long ago.

The chill of sweaty fear cooled him now in this crazy hot heat of the night, just like it did back then, but back then it was during the day, and now, at night, it was refreshing, not just chilling.

Yes.

Refreshing.

Energizing.

The thump-thump-thump in his chest. His foot, no, his toes, tap-tap-tap. With his heart. No sound.

Just feeling.

Feeling each and every expansion, each and every contraction, each and every pulse and pound.

Toes practically wiggling, but actually tapping.

Quicker and quicker.

A dance to doom—that grim bear's doom.

His suede boots let him feel the very soil. How soggy and crumbly it was. Like back when he accidentally stepped on ma's peach pie crumb cake on the windowsill back when Romeo was foolishly trying to climb up through the window and oopsie.

Just like his oopsie now.

Waiting to face a grim bear—on its own terms.

And those ferns confirmed the wind blades extending those claws were all exactly a pace long from each claw.

So Romeo had no other choice now. He raised his harpe.

Did his best not to tremble, but ... no, he mustn't tremble. This gigantic grim bear ... pretend it was a gigantic pa raged beyond rage and ... nonono, a gigantic dwarven *gramps* drunk and raged beyond rage at an insult to all dwarves everywhere.

Yes. A raging gramps. His beard was as furry black as this entire grim bear and both were just as curled fierce.

Yes.

Romeo took a deeeeeep caaalming breath.

A breath full of filthy bear.

And of courage. Enough to ease his trembling. Stop it. His dwarven blood wouldn't allow trembling. Mustn't. It's an insult to all dwarves everywhere.

Yes.

Insult.

Enough to clench his teeth.

Steady himself perfectly. Like a dwarf would.

No.

Should.

"Come on," Romeo said, his voice steady, and even annoyed, "I don't have all day, cubling."

The grim bear ROOOOOOOAAAAAARRRRED again.

But this time, Romeo tensed. Gripped the soil. The filthy gust blasting him.

Trying to shove him back.

But no.

He was as steady as his dwarven gramps.

No.

Steadier.

"I didn't hear that," Romeo said, "Did you whisper something?"

Now the grim bear stomped forward.

"Oh," Romeo said, "Throwing a hissy fit, little cub?"

Its paw raised.

Just like pa raising his own blade. Just like training for the Counter Kill Reversal Technique.

But a zillion times larger.

Faster.

And vicious.

But that thump-thump-thump in his chest, tapping in his toes, everything slowed down.

Slower than a speck of dust falling in stagnant air.

His whole body relaxed, but tensed. Like a pair of springs in a line—his arm, his body—about to be triggered.

About to be released.

The crackle of claw slicing through bark—distant.

The very ground shaking from it—not so distant.

But only a pace above his head.

The smell of moss vaporized with wood.

Confirmed the timing.

He triggered himself. Released the first spring.

Swung up.

Connected.

Released the next spring. Just like pa trained him. Using

the arc of his crescent blade to curve the attack into his own arc, but only slightly.

But just enough.

Sweeping across the whole sharp inner edge.

SKREEEEEEEEEECH!!!

Smacking the center.

And the harpe sung like a harp. The very reason it was called a harpe. After the harp-sound its most dangerous techniques made.

An instant later it was over.

Or so Romeo thought.

CHAPTER 29
VIVIAN

Vivian likey totallies woke up *again*, and this time, she coughed up so much cobweb goo she jostled all bouncy in the giant spider web she was still obviously stuck in.

The spooky rattling of bones was less than before. As if fewer bones were sharing the web with her this time. Just like there was far less water going drip-drip-drip and echoing endlessly from far away.

Vivian was still spread out painfully, like the usual damsel in distress from some spider monster, but now she could move a little.

But just a little bit.

This time, it was darker than before. No ceiling. No walls?

No sign of any of the spooky spires?

Just lots of endless pitch darkness.

Was she in a different spot? The spider web itself glowed

a little bit. A white glow. At least she was totallies likey not in complete and utter darkness again.

And phew, she was still completely dressed for battle too.

Claudia was being nice, especially if they were still likey totallies worried about the necromancer sporing Vivian again and Vivian going evil clawgirl yet once again.

Vivian even flexed her toes and fingers. They were still under her own ... wait, they flexed more and move—without her doing it?

Oh no.

They didn't stop flexing either.

Big oh no.

A familiar chuckle rang out.

A familiar stink of rotting fish.

And of poor tormented fox.

CHAPTER 30
ROMEO

Romeo smirked grimly at his certain victory.

At how proud pa and his gramps would be at this moment.

The smell of moss vaporized with bark, from the bearded oak behind him, from the claw marks no doubt deep within the tree—a stark reminder of what could have happened to him had he failed to pull off the Counter Kill Reversal Technique correctly.

Yet his whole body suddenly gasped. Loud and clear.

Eased up a touch too much.

The ground felt less solid beneath him. Despite the ferns around him being unharmed further.

The grim bear before him ... its arm was gone. Along with a huge chunk of its chest. The stink of blood, bone, and guts vaporized ... ugh, pretty awful.

Yet it ROOOOOAAAAARRRRRED again.

Raised its other arm.

Oh.

SHIT.

Yet Romeo couldn't raise his own sword again. His arms were too weakened from that last technique. He needed more recovery time.

When suddenly—a flash of azure blue by the grim bear's side?

WHAM!

CHAPTER 31
ROMEO

CRACK!

Something big and white smashed into the grim bear. From the side. Halfway down. Folding the bear in half. Sideways in half. Like something heavy and terrible slammed powerfully into its side.

And suddenly—swoosh!

It was gone?

A scream rang out. A gurgle. Its death scream?

The crackle of bramble?

Wait, whoever hit the bear, broke it, flung the gigantic bear into the bramble, and essentially killed it.

All in one blow.

Who ...

"He's not for you to ki—AAAAAHHHH!"

From the blue flash?

That scream, the girliest scream he ever heard.
And a thump. Right into the middle of the shredded ferns.
Wait a moment ...

CHAPTER 32
JULIET

Juliet never ever **ever** wanted to fly any kind of winged lizard—especially a dragon that ... (probably) was her dad—but the wind kept smacking her face and was colder than a dragotroll's heart and whipped her long hair back and back and back, yanking it wild and crazy.

The sun was peeking up over the forest below, making the lower sky as bright red as her claws in her reptilian form. The forest itself was alike a fluffy craggy carpet of dark jagged green—as green as her dragon dad—and far, far, faaaaaar too far below, making her want to cringe once again.

But no.

No more cringing. Her legs already vised the front of this winged lizard's powerful back that still smelled too much like her actual dad, not that she remembered him, like at all, but anyone with a working sense of smell could tell who was related by blood and yet ... how?

Just how could ... it's not like Juliet really knew, actually remembered her mom either but the ... well ... anatomical differences?

Her hand held the spine in front of her like her life depended on it, because it did. No telling what would really happen if she fell and nonono—don't think of falling. Ever. Not this far up. Too far up. Enough that her heart raced as fast as this dragon was flying.

No.

Faster.

What wasn't helping was the furball of a wolf man Jagger was close behind her. Holding a spine behind her and taking a bunch of deep creepy breaths.

Enough to almost make her cringe again.

Almost.

A scream erupted well behind them.

Inhumanly shrill and raptorish.

Juliet glanced backwards. Foolishly glanced back.

And nearly screamed again.

Nearly.

A gigantic hawk, but covered with scaly red feathers, and several tentacles from its head and out of its beak, like countless big slimy tongues ... and three pairs of talons, each one bigger than the other.

Just its next scream stank of predator bird. Too much like the giant terrifying hawks that loved to dive through the thickest trees and prey on her youngest friends back when they were all little wormlings.

All enough to stop her heart for an instant.

Except the dragon let out a laugh?

"No worries over that tentacled razor hawk, little worm-ling," the dragon said, "Daddy's here. You really think a little birdie will get us?"

Juliet grumbled, but didn't tremble ... quite as much either.

Or shiver, as much.

The wind was cold after all. And she was still stuck in this ridiculously revealing leotard.

"Okay, okay," Juliet said, "but we need to lose it or elsssse—"

"We'll do more than lose it," daddy said, "We'll feast on it!"

"Feast?" Juliet said, and ...

The dragon laughed again?

"And see if that boyfriend of yours," the dragon said, "has decent taste too."

"Boyfriend?!?!?!" Juliet said.

More like cried out, but ... Jagger chuckled this time too.

"You're a slow learner," Jagger said, "aren't you?"

Juliet grumbled, but knew better than to say anything this time.

But she did snap her scimitars together, and—

"No need for that," the dragon said, "leave this little birdie to me."

Juliet pouted but ...

"Alright," she said, and slipped her scimitars back in their sheaths.

Just the dragon made a crazy sharp turn.

And flung Juliet off.

Caught her with his talons. Big black eagle-like talons, yet she wasn't crushed or shredded. Not even hurt.

He chuckled again? At her!

"I told you not to let go," the dragon said, "now this is your punishment—looking down the whole way there!"

Juliet gawped and gasped. her heart utterly stopping, because they were so faaaar up ... (eep.)

CHAPTER 33
ROMEO

Romeo blinked, shocked.

More shocked than a dwarf who managed to yank off his own beard.

The forest, silent now. His gasp, a full breath of grim bear gore.

Yet, only paces away, in the straight pathway of shredded ferns ... beyond the slim deep trail that sliced the way to the bearded oak right behind Romeo ...

Flat on her face ... ass-long yet exotically sky-blue hair laid sprawled all over her back (like one of Romeo's many messy mops,) but wow.

That amazingly amazing rear pointed high up in the air, while a gigantic skull-headed war hammer in front of her, in her hands.

And wait, by that rear ... an azure bunny tail?

Woh.

And wait ... azure bunny ears?! Zigzagged but upwards as if shocked stupid.

Wait a moment ... could this girl be ...

She moaned, cried. "Why mmmmmeeeeeee?"

Oh wow. Romeo wasn't sure what to say.

Whether he should respond, or run.

He only heard rumors of rumors of demihumans in dime dreadfuls. They always turned out to be fakes in those books. Not a single real bounty on them either, since even the people who paid those hefty bounties on clawgirls and other monsters questioned the very existence of demihumans. They claimed all sightings proved to be fake, yet ...

If this bunny girl really had sided with the enemies of mankind ...

"No! Azure, you can do better than *this*!"

Uh huh. Giving herself an odd little pep talk seemed oddly cute for bunny girl, but she did save him, so ... Romeo just stayed put and listened.

"You even survived that awful bramble maze!"

Huh? Bramble maze? Where?

(So he could avoid it!)

Face still planted into the ground, she kept whining that pep talk to herself. "And got the perfect mission to prove yourself!"

Um ... mission?

Romeo wasn't sure whether to interrupt or not. That her face was still planted in those ferns' stubs couldn't be pleasant, but his indecision was solved quickly enough.

With an obviously awkward shove and heave upwards,

this girl ... (Azura, was it?) shoved her torso back up, and hips sitting on her knees.

And ... Holy Mother of the Flame Moon, was that girl chest-out heart-stoppingly gorgeous.

Velvet Ruins level of gorgeous.

Even Juliet level of gorgeous.

His heart ... he didn't feel it in his chest. Like it stopped. His breath.

Gone.

Even with her heart of a baby face, even with it covered in tears, gross snot, and countless specks of fern goo. Wow.

Stunningly gorgeous.

As in a life-changing peaches and cream desert for the eyes and loins.

That those bright sparkling lightning blue eyes were so wide and still crying a silent woe-is-me.

(Weirdly cute too.)

That those strawberry sweet lips all pouty but yet determined.

Wow. Romeo ... was still speechless.

That Azura only wore a sky-blue bikini top and matching bikini skirt ... translucent ones at that, so likely some kind of silk, but a stretchy resilient silk.

Yeah.

At least as good as the ones Aunt Tilda had her girls wear for the wealthier patrons and during the biggest festivals.

And this bunny girl's silk outfit was ... wow.

Just wow.

It such fine quality silk it showed a strong silhouette of her dark-blue panties and bra underneath.

Well, her bikini skirt was so short the bottoms of her panties were more than visible anyway.

Still, to add kiss to … to … something, both her bra and panties were also kinda translucent too, so they were also silk of some sort, but not nearly as translucent, but enough to clearly show her stunningly big buxom bosom was truly all breast and no bra enhancement.

Gulp.

Really.

Gulp.

That both her bikini top and skirt were buttoned up with heart-shaped skulls … weird, but the whole enemy to mankind thing … hopefully not really.

(Hopefully.)

Even the crickets and frogs were silent, for now. The murk even seemed less … murky. Could it be sunrise already? No telling how long he'd been wondering this forest.

Azura finally hopped up to her feet. Her boots … and girls cared for their footwear far too much for him to ignore, so that this bunny girl had dark-blue soft-leather boots laced up with more heart-shaped skulls and lined with fluffy azure fur.

Wow.

Who was she? That outfit … not cheap, but not really warrior style either.

Azura even gnashed her teeth at him. Perfectly white and pretty teeth.

"Give me your weapon!" she said, "I saved your life so you owe me!"

Uh huh ... well, better than an outright robbery. Or murder and theft that regular hobgobbles would go for.

Or even slaved clawgirls would do.

"Azura is it?" Romeo said, "I'm Romeo—"

The bunny girl jolted in place.

"You know my name?!" Azura said, "Oh no! WAAAAAAHHHH! Now you can hunt me down and and and ..."

Ooookay now.

Least Romeo was starting to get his second wind by now too. Even in the steaming hot stagnant air, his sweat both chilled and refreshed him now.

So just a little while longer ... no, a good while longer, but once he had a second wind, he'd ... um ... not sure.

Yet.

"Why would I hunt you down?" he said.

"B-b-but," Azura said.

"Since that mission of yours," he said, "you need my weapon but without killing me—"

Azura jolted even more. Her bunny ears going crazy jagged too. As crazy as the crickets and frogs yammering away in the distance.

"You know my mission?!" she said, "I'm ... I'm so going to get eaten now. WAAAAAAHHHHH! B-b-but I must ... must get your weapon anyway. I-I exist to serve the baelzog, s-s-so even if I must d-die ..."

She gulped, shivering. "Please?"

Okay. This was getting weird.

Her bunny ears even drooped as low as they could go. Her eyes opened so big and pleading wide as those beautifully bright lightning-blue eyes could go.

Romeo gulped this time.

It was one thing to fight and kill hordes of ruthless hobgobbles. Or even battle slaved but determined clawgirls.

But a whiny, pathetic, but sweet-natured bunny girl?

Really?

This ...

Shadow Forest was supposed to be filled with ruthless horrors. Like grim bears. Jumping raptors. And worse.

Not ... not ... *this*.

"Azura," Romeo said, "It sounds like you're in deep trouble."

As deep as his own if he didn't recover enough before these crazy weird talks broke down. The stink of the grim bear's gore was a grim reminder of this girls' true strength— and potential brutality.

"Y-yeah," Azura said, hugging her war hammer tight, "if I don't get your weapon in time ..."

"In time for what?" Romeo said.

"I don't knooooow," she said, "but Macker the Cruel had us ... us all ..."

But then suddenly she shut her mouth tight.

The crickets and frogs started yammering again. Nearby too but there. Confirming they didn't sense this bunny girl as too threatening.

Macker .... that's not a hobgobble name, or a clawgirl name, so that left ...

"Let me guess," Romeo said, "That dragotroll had you go through that awful bramble maze."

That jolted Azura badly. So badly she nearly dropped her war hammer, but she caught it quickly, if not awkwardly.

"How'd you knoooooooow?" she said, cringing.

Uh huh. Dime dreadfuls had that kinda of nonsense in spades.

"To trim down your numbers," he said, "Prove who's worthy of ..."

"Of serving that dragotroll alive," she said, cringing even more, "or serving his hobgobbles in death, b-b-but I don't wanna diiiiiiiieeeeeee, b-b-but—"

"Switch sides," Romeo said, "and you don't have to. I'll protect you."

Azura pouted, and gripped her hammer even tighter. "You? But you couldn't even take down a grim bear."

"You think," Romeo said, giving her a sweet smile, "that grim bear is the first monster I've faced these last two days?"

Azura stared at him, then shook her head. "Nonono. But ..."

"You're slaved with spore already?" Romeo said, slumping.

"Spore?" she said, "Oh no. Macker ... that's if I die, or prove unworthy of serving live or or or ... I don't wanna diiiiii-ieeeeee."

Romeo sighed. "None of us do, Sweetheart."

That jolted her again. Ears popping up high and fuzzy.

"What did you call me?" she said, and even bared her perfectly white chompers.

"Um ..." Romeo said, "Sweetheart. Do you—"

Azura snarled. "I'm no useless sweetheart!"

Ooooo crap.

The crickets and frogs suddenly went silent again. The murk seemed even thicker now too, yet also lighter?

Was it really daytime already?

"Nonono," Romeo said, "You're not. Not useless. Not at all."

"I can't kill you," Azura said, "but I *can* cripple you, if I'm careful. You don't want that, right? Just give me your sword, and ... we can be friends, right?"

"Right," Romeo said, "We can be friends—maybe even more."

"M-M-*More?!*" Azura said, more shocked than even Romeo ever expected.

Her ears went zigzagged shocked again.

"Or ..." Romeo said, "you already have a boyfriend?"

"*Boyfriend?!*" Azura said, and her cheeks went ruby red.

Her bunny ears twitching.

Geez, how old was she?

"Unless you're not old enough ..." Romeo said.

Azura growled. "I'm eighteen! More than old enough for ... for ... a boooooyfriend! WAAAAAAAHHH! I have to die before getting my first boyfriend! WAAAAHHHH!"

Oh. Wow.

Everything in the forest was quiet now—outside of Azura herself.

But it could just be his ear were still broken. No, wait.

Why could he hear Azura so well?

He let out a sigh, and tapped his harpe on the ground. That earthy ping—he heard it loud and clear?

His ears weren't broken anymore?

Phew.

Strange, but phew. Maybe the breakage had to do with the grim bear's magic. Once the bear was killed, the magic faded.

"How 'bout this?" Romeo said, "We'll spar. A friendly match. If you win, I give you my harpe, but if I win, you switch sides and become one of girlfriends."

"I-I-I," Azura said, *"**One** of your girlfriends?!?!?! You have more than one*?!"

Her bunny ears ... one popped up shocked straight, and the other went crooked in utter shock.

"Yup," Romeo said, "All beautiful and sweet, like you."

Azura looked even more shocked.

Shocked utterly silent.

Sigh.

Romeo held back a gulp.

"So for the match," he said, "the loser is—"

Suddenly Azura jolted into a battle crouch? Matched with a sneaky smirking and excited face?

"The one," Azura said, raising her hammer over her slim shoulder, "whose ass gets knocked down to the ground."

"Sure," Romeo said, crouching himself, "but—"

"No butts," Azura said, "except yours touching the ground for me!"

And blink!
She vanished.
Too fast to be seen?!

CHAPTER 34
VIVIAN

Vivian strutted along the thin winding path of granite. Razor sharp spires of every color roughly formed a glowing wall to her left. All the spires dripped what looked like water of matching color. Colorful water that streamed down the pathway and over the side into an endless abyss to her right.

An abyss so wide and deep it even ate the echoes.

Every footstep splashed more and more colorful water against her thigh boots. Against her bare thigh. And brrrrr. The water was as freezing cold as her own heart felt right now. How cold and burning depended on the color, and always differed each time, strangely enough.

Yet she couldn't slow down.

Her movement wasn't entirely her own anyway.

Not for ... how long had it been? The icky goo of that spider web still clung her here and there. The spider webs even gooed up her long pink hair. It was bad enough that she could still taste the spider goo in her mouth.

But she was totallies likey under that necromancer hobgobble's control again. Why hadn't the archnofeys stopped her?

Or stopped that hobgobble by now?

No orders echoed through her mind. Just a burning desire to hurry faster and faster over this slim smooth pathway. Forcing her legs to go faster and faster. Despite the steep hazardous abyss to her side, less than a pace away, her arm could even stretch over it—if she could control her arm enough. That abyss ... ughies, it so made her gut cringe cold and painful with fear.

That she didn't ever slip, ever, despite all the water, a miracle in itself.

Since if she fell down the abyss, died, she'd just be revived and, probably, forced to stay at the bottom for eternity as punishment.

Suddenly a rumble rang of ahead of her. Deep enough to rumble her stomach.

She yanked out her pink human-bone scimitars.

Just as a small cluster of red spires speared out horizontally of the wall of spires. Had she been several paces further ... no, don't think like that. Even in sword bouts, never think of that. Ever. Thinking it could make it come true.

But those spires looked even more razor sharp.

Enough to gleam wicked.

Then another cluster closer. Blue. And even quicker.

Then another cluster. Violet. Even quicker.

And closer.

And another. Yellow. So quick.

A blur.

So close it gusted a freezing cold breeze at her.

Vivian crouched.

Leapt

Just a green blur shot out underneath her.

A cluster of green spires.

Gleaming spiraled sharp.

She summoned two pink sabers. Beneath her feet. Landed on their flat edge.

And clank!

Their other side smacked against the sharp green spires.

She leapt again. Flipping midair.

And landed passed all the spires.

"One obstacle down," Vivian said, "And countless more to ..."

RUMBLE!

And so close. The smell of spider?

Vivian summoned seven pink sabers around her protective. Blades alternating up and down, but all ready to slice and dice danger to bits and pieces.

RUMBLE!

Again? Vivian crouched ready for—

Countless overgrown spider webs. Of all colors. All glowing spooky.

Springing out from nowhere.

And yet from everywhere.

But Vivian dodged most of them.

Sliced through the rest.

Every web sliced flung magical sparks of a matching color everywhere. Sparks that signaled magical traps awaited most things that touched it—but not her blades.

Blades that could slice through most magic.

Vivian even giggled, even dodging the sparks, just in case. As slaved as she was, this was still fun, in a way, so lots of giggles. Likey totallies.

"Another obstacle down," she said, "And countless more to go!"

Until a familiar voice added: "But the next, your last!"

CHAPTER 35
ROMEO

Romeo crouched even more ready. His heart thumped the music of battle pure and simple. With a gulp, Romeo steadied his breath, and let the taste in his mouth go sour and dry, yet he remained as eager as ever.

From the lightening murk around him, the frogs and crickets started wailing their usual racket, and the noise was thinning out. But fewer frogs and crickets now.

More bird chirps.

Maybe it was morning after all.

Not a single fern rustled or ripped. None of the fern stubs along the shredded pathways snapped.

The bearded oak behind him guarded his back—for the most part. Just like the stink of grim bear gore in the distance reminded him of the critical stakes of this crazy battle now.

Fighting a heart-wrencher of a stunningly gorgeous

bunny girl—his cheeks were already blazing hotter than the muggy night, no, *morning* air.

Blazed enough that the rest of his body started feeling warmer and warmer.

Beyond sweaty warm.

This was almost as crazy as Velvet fighting alongside him bared utterly naked.

Almost.

Okay, it's pretty a good bit less crazy than Velvet but—no.

Focus.

Gulp.

Another deeeeeep breath.

Caaaaalm.

His heart. Thump thump thump.

A breeze. Into his face. Full of fern.

No. Think.

Where would the bunny girl come from?

Nowhere obvious.

Not from the front. Not from the side.

Behind?

Above?

Below?

No. If crippling him is the goal … but a direct strike mangled and killed a full-grown grim bear.

No chance he'd survive a direct blow.

But an indirect blow … and what's the most obvious—ah!

An explosion boom. Behind him.

The bearded oak. Musty wood everything suddenly.

Just as Romeo leapt. Rolled—no.

Flew.

His harpe. Into the ground. Flipping him. Swirling him.

Pa. Another technique: Whirlwind Woosh. How many times. Did Romeo flop, flipping or spinning, and needed to turn around the situation.

And very suddenly.

The wind. Roaring in his ears cold. Frigid. Like the fear of losing. Losing his sword.

It's his only hope of saving his new clawgirl girlfriends.

But the world still. Spun and spun. Dizzy. And dizzier.

A blue flash. Blur. By the shattered bearded oak.

And coming closer.

And closer.

And closer.

No time for Whirlwind Woosh.

Or any technique.

But pa warned him: never over-rely on techniques. Especially in close-quarters battle.

Heart thumping music. Too slow for that kind of battle. Far too slow.

Time for something clever.

And dangerous.

CHAPTER 36
FLEUR

Fleur was breathing far too slow and unsteady to use any special techniques—yet. Her heart raced far too fast to follow, to time the technique, any technique. The hot muggy air wasn't helping, but no excuses.

Battles weren't about fairness.

The three-eyed crow on her slim shoulder pinched her tight with its small sharp claws. Its eyes didn't seem to glow as bright, but the thick winding branch was ... easier to see now too.

Just like the many winding thick branches around her. Now a clear solid brown. From sunlight peeking through the thick canopy. The thick clusters of leaves. Plenty of places for Velvet to hide too.

Feather Fleur from behind.

Fleur took another deep breath. There. A crispness to the hot muggy air. A hint of morning.

And a hint of almonds of vanilla?

He-he.

Unlike Vanessa, Velvet never figured out how to hide her scent any better than Fleur did.

Fleur took another breath. Let her heart beat as fast as the songbirds were now chirping here and there.

Chirps Velvet loved to imitate. Use to distract and defeat others with.

But Velvet wasn't the backstabbing type either. She'd want Fleur to know who defeated her, to see that look of despair. Just like when they were teens and they hunted down grim bear after grim bear and and and ...

Gulp.

No. Fleur was fighting how Velvet expected her to fight. Sending Claudia away. Facing Velvet here. Alone.

No.

Two vs two, and Romeo couldn't be as rested as Fleur was. He must have traveled a good ways tonight.

So Fleur cackled. "You really think I'd—"

Violet bolts flashed before her.

Smashed into the branch right by her feet.

Velvet would move swiftly to a new position. Turning to look. No use. Listening was the only hope. Carefully and intensely.

But her heart—thump thump thump.

So Fleur flipped backwards. Keeping her eyes as open as she could. Watching the leaves and branches swirled by.

She landed horizontally on the trunk.

Crouched. Focused.

Sliding down slow and steady.

A quiet rustle below …

Below her! Velvet utter nude? The same color as the bark! Clever!

Fleur loosed a rapid rain of icicle-enhanced bolts at her.

But Velvet vanished just as quickly again.

A tanned brown blur.

Zigzagging between the thick branches.

Almost unpredictable.

Almost.

Fleur slid down to her original branch. Hopped to her feet.

Loosed several bolts.

Seemingly spread randomly.

Crack!

Crack!

Crack!

Bolt shot down by Velvet, midair, forcing her to stop zigzagging.

Long enough for Vanessa to loose several bolts at Velvet from behind?!?! (Fleur forgot about Vanessa completely! (Oopsie.))

But those bolts just barely missed.

But not Fleur's next bolts.

They all exploded?

No. They all smashed into Velvet's scimitar bow.

Felling Velvet anyway. The crows everywhere flocking around her.

Her scream.

Like an icicle to Fleur's own heart.

But that crow cackling in her ear …

Until a bright violet explosion ripped through all the crows. Vaporizing them. Black and violet smoke.

Smelling of roasted crow, and that almond and vanilla of Velvet.

"Nisssse one, Fleur," Velvet said, "You're worthy of being saved—so catch me if you can!"

"I vell do more than catch you, zhees time, no?" Fleur said, and followed that blur of bright violet serpent as quick as she could.

Her heart pumping more than just fear this time.

But sugary excitement.

CHAPTER 37
ROMEO

Clever and dangerous—to first swirl around more and more.

Just like pa ruthlessly taught Romeo so many times before. The world spun around and around, just like it did so many times before. From endless winding branches thick with leaves to dark leafy soil full of rocks and ferns and back again to branches.

The wind smashed right in his face. Warm yet cooling. Like falling into one of ma's best desserts by clutzy accident again. It forced him to squint more and more.

Focus on his heart racing more and more.

That thump-thump-thump of his heart, timing both his arms going 'round-'round-'round.

The blue blur nearly on him. Azura. That war hammer, its giant skull head aimed at … at … above him!

To smack him down with the after-gust.

But both his arms. Completely under his control.

Timing. Completely under control.

The war hammer. So slow.

Yet so unstoppable.

Till his harpe caught the ground. Hooked it.

Yanked him to a stop.

Yet flipping him around. His arm tightening.

Swooshing him well underneath the hammer.

His boots.

Right into her gut.

Her gasp.

Her last—for now.

Or so he thought.

CHAPTER 38
VIVIAN

Vivian hesitated at the rope bridge woven from thick spider threads. Three solid ropes, creaking soft and gooey. Two for hands and one for feet.

Worse, each was woven from the same kind of colorful spider threads that the previous traps were made of. Each color signaled a different kind of magical trap awaited the fool who dared touch it.

Or even cut it with the wrong kind of blade.

A blade unlike hers.

Worst of all, the narrow pathway ended here. The spires had long since vanished. Not even drip-drip-drip rang out here. No cold water.

Nothing. Just freezing cold air.

And a thin smooth pathway that glowed a dim but solid blue now.

A glow that only spread out a pace around her.

And never moved backwards.

Ever.

At least whenever she wobbled—almost losing her footing here and there—the glow never edged backwards, it only edged forward.

Went forward when she did.

The pathway itself had shrunk narrower and narrower. By now it was barely as wide as a slim little deer path. Sure, the pathway split and forked a few times, but the necromancer controlled with route Vivian went down, yet now, was this rope bridge trap up to her?

No instructions on how to pass it?

And that familiar voice before, by the first spider web trap ... it sounded like Fleur, but there had been plenty of other traps since then. Maybe it wasn't just another trick. To lower her guard, even if the necromancer controlling Vivian wouldn't likey ever even allow that sort of thing.

"Um ..." Vivian said, "Master? What should I do now?"

She heard a chuckle with her own mind.

Think, clawgirl, think, the necromancer said, *Or must I guide your very breath too?*

"I ..." Vivian said.

To think, the necromancer said, *your kind slaved and controlled mine for so long ...*

That verbal jab ...

"I never called your kind stupid," Vivian said, "or—"

But you thought it! the necromancer said, *And used us as expandable fodder. My clan as expandable fodder. Now you serve us! In life and death!*

Oh yippie. A vengeful—

Agony erupted throughout her whole body. Freezing it solid. So bad she couldn't even whimper. Even breathe. It was a solid hard cringe that filled her vision with stars.

And was gone just as quickly.

A *taste,* the necromancer said, *of what's to come—if you dare ever think badly of me again.*

Vivian gulped, shivering. "Yes, Master."

Good, the necromancer said, *I don't need you conscious for this part anyway. Sleep, and when you awaken, little clawgirl,* ***if*** *you awaken ...*

The necromancer's chuckles echoed through Vivian's mind like her own mind had become a vast empty cavern.

As if Vivian totallies was the airhead she pretended to be.

CHAPTER 39
ROMEO

With splinters of the smashed bearded oak flying his way, with his own body spinning and yanked to its fullest, with the winding branches thick with leaves above him, the ferns below, and Romeo doubling kicking that heart-wrencher of a stunningly gorgeous bunny girl in the slim bare gut ...

Except she held onto her hefty war hammer. And it carried her forward even more.

And more.

Forcing his legs to give.

Bend.

And PLOMP!

Onto the ground. Both of them

More like his him onto her leather boots. Those skulls lacing up her boots bit his butt cheeks like little dull spikes.

Painful enough to get a yelp out of him.

THUMP!

Her war hammer landed right beside them both. Savaging more ferns along the way.

She gasped again. More like rasped.

"I ... I ... *lost?!?!*" she said.

"Yup," he said, his thighs on hers, no so bad either, "and no take-backs."

"Take ... backs?" she said, "I ... I ... WAAAAAAAAHHHHH! I'm so going to die now!"

She cried up to the canopy. Her bunny ears so down and drooping.

So Romeo rolled forward. Vising her lush hips gentle. And gave her an even more gentle hug.

She even smelled of cute bunny this close up.

"No you won't," he said, "I'll protect you. Like I'll protect all my girlfriends."

"G-g-girlfriends?!?!?" she said, trembling, "I'm ... I'm just a concubine now, aren't I? here to serve and sex you and and and—"

"Pervy rabbit," Romeo said, "but if you want sex so badly, I'm not one to say no ..."

This time Azura gasped so shocked, and her blush turning her so red ... as red as the cherry pie he'd one day bake for his girlfriends.

Especially this weird but sweet bunny girl.

"Y-y-you 'll ... really ..." she said, and gulped. "B-b-but ..."

Romeo smooched her right on the strawberry sweet lips. Stroked her supersoft azure bunny girls. Their whole long length.

And kissed her lips again.

Her big lightning blue eyes so wide and shocked and pleading that ... sigh.

"But if you don't want to," he said, "you don't have to. Really. I—"

She smooched him back. "I-I-I want to. D-d-don't want die a v-v-virgin.

And kissed him again.

And again.

Slipping her slim hands up under his vest. Slipping it above his head. And her palms fondled his chest. Rubbed his solid pecks with cute but gross drooling glee.

So he unbuttoned her silky smooth bikini top. Heart-shaped skull after skull after skull. Slipping her top off.

Her bra top off and ... Holy Mother of the Flame Moon, were those ... those breasts ... **huge** and and and ... his hands. Rubbing their soft supple and and and gulp.

Azura wasn't the only one drooling now.

CHAPTER 40
JULIET

With so many branches swooshing passed her, right below her practically, faster than fast, with the wind yanking her hair as much as those branches would soon tangle it, her mouth went sour.

All too sour.

But daddy's claws holding her were as gentle as overgrown eagle talons could be, so maybe, yeah, he was her daddy, since smell, hard to fake and and and—sigh.

At least the sun was out again. No more pitch icky darkness.

For now.

The dragon laughed again. "So there he is."

"Who?" Juliet said.

This time both the dragon and the furball known as Jagger laughed out loud.

"Guess," the dragon said, "In fact, it's time the two of you go see him."

"Go see ... AAAAAAAHHHHHHH!"

That dragon let go of her!

Dropped her.

And she was falling and falling and oh crap.

CHAPTER 41
ROMEO

Romeo didn't his best to not to drool too much, and failed badly, in the best way possible, since focusing on his legs, not how they vised Azura's lush hips so gently but how his shins and feet were soaked from the soggy dark soil.

Underneath the lusting bunny girl smell, was grim bear ick and earthy musty forest. Never mind all the musty from the bearded oak, that was still creaking from the damage Azura dealt to it earlier.

Enough that he really should glance its way but Azura, no, her breasts were a truly an amazing sight to behold.

Like ... like ... words couldn't describe ... heart racing stupid for the best possible reason. Enough that he rubbed and squeezed them as much as she was rubbing and squeezing his own pecks.

They both giggled so lusty at each other that … that … another smooch was practically a no-brainer.

No. His brain was shutting off just like his pants were coming off. His boots too. Off, off, and off.

While he unbuttoned her bikini skirt. Skull after skull after skull.

Her giggle as he slipped her dark-blue panties down, down, and down … kissing her lush legs down, down, and down. And now, she wasn't the only one blushing superhot and redder than … than …

GULP.

With another gasp he was in her. Fitting inside her like a warm glove on a winter day. Her back curled, shoving her soft massive breasts against him even more, as he held her hips and pumped more and more and more. They panted together, more and more and more and—

Romeo released his seed, just as Azura screamed out her last pant.

And a girlie grumble erupted behind them.

"Geez," Juliet said, "You'll fuck any pretty thing that falls for you, won't you?"

CHAPTER 42
MACKER THE CRUEL

acker the Curl just had to chuckle.

Despite the boiling stew of chopped demi-humans and human blood in the black iron cauldron before him ...

Despite the sweet smell of the dark-pink and toxic black-berries throughout the bramble maze ...

Even over a mile away, the smell of human lust, of demi-human rabbit lust, as he expected of such a weak-willed rabbit, but well over a few dozen more rabbit girls survived the maze and his axe.

Another couple dozen more tigers, bears, and foxes all together.

All watching him in full attention. Standing tall by the bramble wall. Still shocked terrified at how many of their companions were slaughtered by Macker himself.

Some of their remains regrown and reanimated to serve that hobgobble necromancer in death rather than alive.

Macker motioned to the crows above him.

Time for the next step.

A double trap.

For both the boy and those wrenched traitors that soon would serve in death rather than in life.

CHAPTER 43
ROMEO

At least the morning air was still muggier than a starving bandit, because otherwise Romeo standing bare utterly naked beside a bare utterly naked bunny girl, and well, even his feet felt how the ground was still soggy warm and leafy and kinda yucky that, wow, Azura must have really wanted some manhood in her to not mind laying down on this soggy soil.

More than not mind. To savor it.

On a deer path no less!

Enough that the bearded oak creaking loudly behind them now was ... well ... maybe they should go check on it and make sure the tree wouldn't actually fall on them.

The birds chirped away as if cheering them all on to go happy threesome next. No need to stand amidst the ferns.

Savor his manliness to the ladies.

His ladies.

But Juliet was looming gloomy a few paces in front of them both. Her arms folded over her ample chest. Her heart of a face pouting peeved at them both. She even was tapping her foot, in a thigh boot.

That she was dressed, actually dressed, unlike Romeo and Azura, but she was in the usual clawgirl getup, especially that sexy lightning blue leotard with suggestive pink lightning all over it ...

Juliet huffed. "I'm not spored."

"I know," Romeo said, "I'd be so dead if you were."

"You and that bunny girl," Juliet said, "I know what you're thinking. I can smell it, but we don't have time to do a threesome. Really."

"Aaaaaawwww," Romeo said, "You sure?"

"Pretty please?" Azura said, going all cutie pie bunny girl, ears all droopy and eyes going big and pleading.

Juliet tsked, shaking her head.

"I ... I am tempted," Juliet said, "but we're not alone. And I don't mean the birds. Jagger come out!"

Silence—except for the excited songbirds.

Romeo shrugged. "Jagger? Who ... my sword!"

"Huh?" Juliet said, "Where ..."

But Romeo pointed at the slit of a hole his sword had left when he dug it into the ground.

Azura gasped. "Oh nonono! I'm the one who's supposed to snatch it. I-I-I WAAAAAAAAHHHH! I'm so going to—"

Juliet slapped Azura?

"Enough bawling your eyes out, you idiot," Juliet said, "You have ears and I have smell. I can smell that bastard betrayed us. How he hid it till now ... never mind. Let's get that sword back."

"B-b-but," Azura said.

SLAP!

Juliet slapped her again? Romeo ... wasn't sure what to do right now.

Even the birds weren't chirping as much now.

"And if you even *think* of betraying us," Juliet said, "I'll scent it and slit your throat with my scimitars. No. Chop your head off. Understand?"

Azura gasped. "I-I-I ..."

SLAP!

Azura whimpered, nodded. "I ... understand."

And she slumped.

"But how ... I ..." Azura said, "if we get spored and and and ..."

"No more time to waste," Juliet said, "the hunt starts now. And be careful. He's a wolf man. As in full furball wolf on two legs."

Azura gasped. "A demibeast?! B-b-but—"

SLAP!

Juliet slapped Azura again.

Except Azura slapped Juliet back this time.

"Stop slapping meeeee!" Azura said, "Demibeasts, they're-they're even more even more dangerous than-than-than ..."

SLAP!

Again. Juliet slapping Azura. At this rate there'd be a full-fledged cat fight at the worse possible moment.

Sigh. Romeo knew better than to jump in.

Yet.

He just stood there silent and ready.

Except suddenly behind Juliet ... something Romeo never thought actually existed.

A dragon?!

CHAPTER 44
FLEUR

Some sugary excitement powered Fleur to leap passed countless thick clusters of leaves full of spider webs and worse. She landed solidly and loudly on winding branch to winding branch, mossy tree to mossy tree, while savoring the songbirds chirping their fears of her to their hidden companions.

Just like back when she was a wormling. Out hunting in the treetops because the ground was far too dangerous—yet.

Except her prey was the deadly Velvet Ruins. Bare naked so she could blend more easily into the lightening murk.

Even in her reptilian form.

With bright violet scales over most of her body. her hair was still as lovely black as her heart was supposed to be, as black as any clawgirl's heart should be, according to their creators, the baelzog and their minions.

Except her claws were dark purple. Her smirking lips too. Her claw power—not just explosive violet flames.

But a deadly paralysis if struck.

Fleur was a dozen paces behind Velvet.

No time to fire more bolts at Velvet. Just pursuing her was as much as Fleur could handle right now.

But back years ago, before Fleur became so timid, she could do both.

And easily.

Maybe it was time to try—ah! The three-eyed crow! It pinched her shoulder. Claws digging in painfully. Cawed threateningly.

"Not just try …" the crow said, "Do—even if you must die. Death will not stop us."

Fleur gulped. "Yessss, Master."

She leapt again. Tried aiming mid-leap.

And barely managed to land again.

Nearly stumbled off the branch.

Another pinch?!

"Fall if you must!" the crow said, "Nothing teaches better than a harsh death!"

Fleur gulped again. "Yesss, Master."

She leapt again. Heart racing faster than during her first grim beat hunt. The air gusting into her face too strong—but she didn't dare blink.

Not yet.

She whipped her bow in Velvet's direction.

Fired a barrage of icicle-enhanced bolts.

All missing.

A velvety laugh broke out.

"Not even able to aim yet?" Velvet said, "How sad ... but we're almost there."

Velvet even cackled. Going even faster. Getting even further ahead now.

"And a few crows won't stop me," Velvet said, "or a few bolts."

And the worse thing was—she was right.

Yet this crow pinched Fleur in the shoulder even more painfully.

"Fail again," the crows said, "and Master shall control you personally."

Fleur gulped again. Her body becoming as chilly as her own icicles.

"Yessss, Master," she said, and leapt.

Aimed.

Fired.

All midair. All ...

Bang!

Bang!

Bang!

All hit!

But got deflected. By that scimitar bow.

"Better," Velvet said, with a velvety laugh, "but too predictable."

"B-b-but," Fleur said, "not for long, no?"

"We'll see ..." Velvet said, and laughed even more scornfully this time.

But Fleur, her breath, her heartbeat, it matched Velvet's

pace. Her laugh. Her leaps. Even the thick bangs of Velvet's talons landing, clinging for an instant on those branches.

Her next leap Velvet gasped. "Vivian?!"

That playfully bubbly laugh. Vivian was caught too?

Her shoulder. The pain. No!

Fleur aimed at Velvet. Clangs rang out. A flash of pink. A familiar rosy pink with pale pink hearts. Vivian! And her pink floating sabers? Fighting Velvet? Velvet was so acrobatic and beautiful and *distracted*.

Perfect!

Fleur fired.

Velvet never noticed—until it was too late. And she screamed. In pain.

Fell.

"Follow her!" the crow said, "And finish her off!"

Fleur nodded, her heart icier than her own icicle-enhanced bolts.

"Yesss, Master," Fleur said, and headed down.

Her leaps this time. Graceful and deadly.

No hesitation now.

The real Fleur was back—at least on the outside.

CHAPTER 45
ROMEO

Romeo somehow managed to gulp. His mouth was more sour than when Aunt Tilda washed it with lemon juice whenever he dared speak of adventure wherever she could hear him.

Even that time only a week ago.

But far back in the murk, murk that was lightening from the morning light, making the bearded oaks before Romeo, beyond the wide pathway his Slash-o-Boom Technique had made, about a dozen paces, beyond more ferns, where more bearded oaks were, on the lowest branch, a thick winding but craggy branch …

It couldn't be …

Yet Romeo could even smell the winged lizard from here. The serpent stink, and even the strong stink of flame and smoke from its nostrils. The kind of smoke that was even more biting than any smoky fireplace.

Its tail was curled tight around the branch and cracking it.

"Um ... Juliet?" Romeo said, and did his best not to gulp too loudly.

Juliet only tsked. "The dragon? I know. He's my *dad*."

"Ooo," Romeo said, "WHAT?!?!"

This time even dragon tsked loud and clear.

"I'd eat the boy for cheating," the dragon said, "but you already agreed to share him with ... how many other girls?"

Juliet grumbled. "*Not* now. We need that sword."

Awkward so ... Romeo nodded, and finally got dressed. Quickly. Almost as quickly as Azura did.

But he did slip his arm around Azura's slim waist. Gave her another looooong smooch.

A smooch she moaned for as much as he did.

"Azura," Romeo said, "You're fast. Super-fast. I need you to catch up to that wolf man and—"

Azura jolted, trembling. "I know. I know. B-b-but promise you'll come save me. I-I-I won't last long against a wolf. Any wolf. Really. Pleeeeease?"

"Of course," Romeo said, "Right Juliet?"

Juliet grumbled, but then gave both Romeo and Azura a cozy snug hug.

"Of course," she said, "Welcome aboard Azura. We'll hurry up and take him down together."

Azura gulped loud and clear. "O-o-okay."

After another snug hug, Azura grabbed her oversized skull-headed war hammer, perked her ears high up, and dashed off.

So fast she was a blue blur.

Just as another scream rang out. From above them, and ...
Romeo gasped. "Velvet?!"

CHAPTER 46

ROMEO

For a horrible moment the scream shot through the forest, silencing all the songbirds, echoing around the bearded oaks as if seeking a savior. It even jolted Romeo, making him stumble backwards off the deer path, the very path slicing through the ferns toward the damaged bearded oak.

To fumble through the ferns.

Amidst the smell of fern goo and earthy soil, was now the smell of blood. Serpent blood. Hinting of that familiar almonds of vanilla.

Clawgirl blood!

Romeo gulped. Clenched his fists. No harpe but ... no.

No excuses. That empty gash in the ground, where his harpe once was, that was no excuse at all.

Pa taught Romeo plenty. Romeo often used the harpe—a family heirloom—especially when starting to learn a technique, but they just as often used practice swords. As in carved straight branches of oak. Nothing special.

So he should be able use the same techniques wielding only a piece of wood.

Even a twig. From many scattered on the ground. Really, but ... its cutting power ... worthless unless ...

"Juliet," Romeo said, "I need one of your scimitars."

Juliet tsked. "By time you asked."

And she handed it to him quickly, without delay.

Its pink handle felt so soft yet so firm—like some perfectly carved ivory, despite him knowing it was human bone of some sort. Its guard was well formed and very protective. While its blade curved nice and wicked. Its lightning blue coloring and decorations a very nice touch.

And the balance—even more amazing. Just like its weight. Enough to be solid but not tiring.

Romeo never thought human bones could be used to make such amazing swords.

Juliet growled. "Stop admiring my sword and—"

"Good point," Romeo said, "I'll admire your blades later. Time to hurry. Velvet needs us."

They both dashed toward the source of the scream. Dozens of paces away. The murk hiding it, but just barely.

"You mean Velvet Ruins?" Juliet said, running as fast as Romeo easily, all because of her extra height, "You even snagged her? Wow. I ..."

Mid-stride, Romeo gave her a cozy side-hug and peck on her lovely cheek.

"Another girlfriend for you too," Romeo said, and with a

gentle smile, "A pack of close friends. Real friends. No more loneliness."

Juliet grimaced, but packed his lips back, mid-stride.

"And another lover for you," Juliet said, and dashed even faster, "Another lover rival I won't lose to either!"

Far behind them that dragon laughed out loud.

"That's my girl," the dragon said.

Juliet screamed, waving her hand and sword high up. "You could at least help us!"

"My old bones need a rest," the dragon said, "Maybe a bit later. Once you've grown some more."

"I've grown enough!" Juliet said, and still waved her hand and sword, as if that would do anything now.

Romeo wisely said nothing. Pa would have probably done the exact same. Only intervening if things when too badly. The youngings gotta learn the hard way, as pa would say, and this dragon seemed to think the same as pa.

But if the dragon did need to intervene, would he approve of Romeo as his daughter's lover? Especially since she wasn't the only clawgirl Romeo was claiming as a lover.

Well, if pa had a daughter and ... oh crap.

That dragon would probably eat him—or something worse.

A lot worse.

Better-not-think-of-it worse.

"Velvet!" Romeo cried out, "Hold on! We're coming!"

CHAPTER 47
VIVIAN

Vivian awoke, standing on a thick branch so full of moss she could taste it, except agony from something binding her hands together tight and, as if … there were spikes through them, binding them together. The pain, the agony flooded almost all her vision with stars.

Ughies.

It totallies almost made her whimper too, but she refused to, likey, even yelp.

Squinting, she was awake now and refused to embrace helplessness, or even dare ask that necromancer for help again. It was still murky around her, but plenty of lighter now. Brown bark was everywhere. Well, except where there were thick clusters of leaves and thick layers of moss.

And lots more winding branches. Even thicker and wider and far more mossy tree trunks here and there.

A deep breath and lots of musty mossy meh, but those songbirds even chirped in a distance.

Ah! Yay! Back in Shadow forest.

She wasn't underground anymore!

The smell of almonds and vanilla, with a strong hint of blood and serpent ... wait a moment, not just any serpent, but clawgirl serpent?

Oh noes.

Oh yes!

A hallow but manly voice, in her head?

The blood of beautiful warrior girls is the best! Feed me MORE! Feed me the best, and I may forgive your failures.

Not the necromancer but ... ack!

"My hands!" Vivian cried out.

In her hands was a wicked scimitar of blood red. Like an evil deer antler curved drastically and sharpened even worse. The black hilt and dark red handle both had totallies swallowed her hands together into a spiky hard ball of agony.

A chuckle erupted in her mind. The hallow but manly voice again.

I am the Savage Sword of Shadow Forest! Rejoice and despair! You will feed me your lovely friends and then yourself, and such a delicious feast you will be.

"Never!" Vivian said, her voice so weak, "I ... I'd rather—"

The necromancer chuckled in her head now.

*Serve live or dead. The choice is **mine**.*

Another scream rang out. Below. Well below her.

And then, right below Vivian was ... Fleur?

The blade hungered for more girl flesh.

Clawgirl flesh. For Fleur?!

The hallow but manly voice growled even nastier.

No. I refuse to serve the undead, filthy necromancer. Their taste is awful. Worse than your spore. This vile pathetic girl is bad enough—unless I feast on her loved ones and savor her agony to the end—her true end.

The necromancer chuckled. *So be it. Slaughter them all. Painfully and in utter agony. And savor that blonde girl below. Her use is nearing an end.*

"But," Vivian. said, "the baelzog ... didn't you want to free them?"

Both of them chuckled knowingly now, but neither bothered to answer her.

CHAPTER 48
ROMEO

Within the ocean of ferns cut in half by his Slash-o-Boom last night, only a few paces before the towering wall of bramble with its strangely sweet dark-pink blackberries, and barely a dozen paces away from several of the bearded oaks, Romeo spotted the gap in the ferns where Velvet must have fallen.

Dashing as fast as he could toward it.

Juliet right behind him now.

That hint of serpent blood, along with the warm wind gusting into his face, carrying with it a solid whiff of that familiar almond and vanilla, Romeo gulped. His mouth sour at what he would find.

But his new blade, Juliet's blue bladed and pink handled scimitars, was out and ready to defend Velvet to the death.

If death had not already claimed her ...

A moan rang out from the gap.

"Romeo?" Velvet rasped. "Please ..."

"Are you hurt?" Romeo called out, dashing to her even faster, leaving Juliet behind now.

"No, not that," Velvet said, her voice getting more velvety again, "My scales, they've been ... damaged. I'm ..."

But Romeo didn't stop. He reached her and ... her stunningly gorgeous and bare utterly naked body was now, her skin was now stunningly gorgeous bright violet scales. Her claws, eagle-style talons for both hands and feet, they were dark purple, just like her long lush dark hair now.

Except along the side away from him her gorgeous scales were blemished. Several splotches of bruised blackish. She clearly tried to cover it with her arm, but no, it was all too visible.

"Romeo ..." Velvet said, her gorgeously violet eyes downcast as she sat up, "I'm hideous now. Until I molt again I ... I will soon. Don't worry, but ... ah!"

Romeo hugged her tight. "You're alright."

"Of course, you fool ..." Velvet said, her quiet voice so velvety, yet the smile on her dark purple lips very much reached her eyes.

Fleur chuckled above them? "But not for long, no?"

"Watch out!" Velvet said, and rolled over him. Shielding him with her body.

Bang!

Bang!

Bang!

Velvet gasped. Tensing terribly. Clearly in more pain than she sounded.

And with the smell of winter. The sudden chill in the air.

So it was an icicles barrage. Saving him already, when he came to save her.

"Velvet …" Romeo said, and kissed her full on the lips.

"Who said you could kiss me?" Velvet said, but then kissed him back even more passionately. "Now we're even."

Juliet yelped. "Vanessa! You bitch!"

That jolted Romeo. "We—"

Velvet pecked his lip again. "I know. Save Fleur. Leave Vanessa to me."

Romeo nodded, and Velvet was off.

Just as another barrage of icicles flew down at him.

CHAPTER 49
ROMEO

Romeo didn't hesitate.

That breeze of almonds of vanilla vanishing, but far from the last time, just like the taste of Velvet on his lips warming them, making the soggy ground against his back a blissful reminder of what would come later.

As long as they all survived. Free and save.

The ferns curling, swaying above him didn't block his whole view.

Just narrowed it down to the sharp blue icicles speeding his way.

His scimitar, one of two blue blades Juliet once wielded, was up, and ready to block.

BANG!

BANG!

BANG!

Romeo gasped. The pain. His chest.

The power behind those icicles was too much. If he hadn't been laying down. If he hadn't been on soft earthy soil. Had there been a single pebble in the wrong spot under him ...

He couldn't risk blocking those icicles again.

A couple dozen paces above him, on a thick branch over hanging him was the gorgeous blonde clawgirl Fleur. In that blue leotard. Staring down at him as cold as her own icicles.

"R-R-Romeo," she said, "s-s-sorry but, you must die."

His heart thumped in his ears. The music of battle. If adventure. Of exactly what Aunt Tilda was most afraid of.

Yet the pain. His whole body. It was too limp.

Weakened.

She aimed her scimitar bow at him. A three-eyed crow clinging tight to her shoulder, yet blended all too well into the murk above, while the evil thing cawed right into her ear.

With plenty more crows around her.

All cawing in certain victory.

But the pain in her eyes looked as great as the pain in his whole body.

So Romeo clenched his teeth.

How many times had pa smacked Romeo so badly in a bout that he went limper, was weakened, but refused to give up?

Never give up.

How many times had Romeo himself mistaken Fleur's stuttering coldness with haughty distain rather than her true feeling, nervous affection?

Her heart thumped at his stupid denseness.

At him failing her again.

But not this time.

Just like in those bouts. He could do it.

Romeo tensed his whole body.

Released a flying slash.

But only gasped the technique's name.

Just as Fleur loosed another bunch of icicles down at him.

Icicles that suddenly shattered.

Fleur leapt—but not fast enough.

Her scream. Fumble midair. Her outfit shattered. Just like the crow on her shoulder. And a bunch more behind her.

No time to leer at her beautifully nude body.

Romeo leapt to his own feet. Pain shocked his whole body. Jolting him so badly he could barely breath.

He even fumbled back to his knees. The ground barely catching him. the softness of the soil not enough to dull the pain in his knees.

"Fleur," he rasped, his vision fading.

Yet Fleur tensed. Grimaced.

And caught herself midair, as if steadying herself?

Even landed on the branch like a feline. A feline on the hunt.

She even giggled now. Lusty yet hungry, as if hungry for more fighting?

"Romeo," she said, "Time for me to save you, no?"

But Romeo couldn't even gasp a reply.

CHAPTER 50
FLEUR

Fleur was free.

Really, really free again.

All thanks to Romeo. His sacrifice. His near death, but she refused to let him die.

No.

On the mossy thick branch, despite being completely naked now. Her hands empty. Her scimitars fallen somewhere on the ground.

No.

She posed like the many hunting felines she secretly cared for. Felines Boss Tilda only humored because they were all amazing mousers. Every single one of them.

No time to search for her scimitars. Let her outfit regenerate.

Time to go naked clawgirl. Full reptilian battle bitch.

Just like Velvet was.

Her skin turned into sky-blue scales. Her hands and feet talons with lightning blue claws. Her hair became as azure as those tropical oceans she saw only in painting, and yearned to one day see for herself.

Her teeth, fangs, and ready to protect her beloved boyfriend.

To the death.

CHAPTER 51
VIVIAN

The moment her entire outfit shattered once more, Vivian didn't know whether to totallies hate that perverted Romeo, or likey love him even more.

The chuckle of that necromancer vanished instantly. Just like all the crows shattering around here. Crows Vivian only now noticed. At their awful and well-deserved end.

But the chuckle of this sword binding her hands ... stayed?

By time, the Savage Sword said, *A worthy wielder is below. Feast on the clawgirl below you, and the others, and then—*

Vivian snarled. Finally free to react.

Vent at this wretched stupid blade.

"I'm unworthy?!" Vivian said, "You ... you ..."

The pain in her hands, the agony inflicting countless stars blinding her ... but this time she didn't tried to pry the sword off.

No.

This time she clutched it ever tighter. Squeezing her hands together. No matter how many stars flooded in her vision.

Her feet trembled.

How many times had she defeated Romeo?

Sure, Boss Tilda insisted Vivian win, but it wasn't like Romeo simply keeled over. Vivian **forced** him to keel over plenty of times.

And no patron ever forced her to keel over.

She always lost when the moment was right—and *never* **ever** before.

"You want worthy, you worthless sword?" Vivian said, and summoned all thirteen of her pink sabers.

Smashed them all together—into this worthless hunk of magical metal.

Squeeeeezing them together.

CRACK!

CRACKLE!

And … her hands were free. Her sabers were now … their blades were a wickedly spiraled rosy pink. Their handles now a stylish reddish pink. And the cupped guard a rose red.

This time she heard an annoyed grunt in her mind, and the hallow but manly voice wasn't as manly now.

Fine, the Savage Sword said, *I'll give you a chance to prove your worth—and spare your loved ones … for now.*

This time, it was Vivian who chuckled.

Especially when Vanessa screamed at Fleur.

And Fleur immediate replied, "Fleur Killjoy was your death, no?"

CHAPTER 52
ROMEO

The murk had brightened enough that it had to be noon by now, and yet, even with the bearded oak and its thick moss softening the solid bumpy roots and rough trunk, making a cozy but awkwardly makeshift seat, Romeo couldn't help but enjoy the rosy fragrance of Vivian as she once again slept with her back to his chest, her rear resting against his crotch, and their legs entwined together.

Something Aunt Tilda would of never ever humor, ever, especially after one of their matches.

The song birds cheered their lovey dovey reunion on, as much as his other clawgirls giving them some space to enjoy each other, since they were interrupted last night and sigh.

The breeze was nice and warm and refreshing.

Except for the heart-wrenchingly gorgeous bunny girl Azura leaning and drooling on his shoulder, as she whimpered sorry, sorry, sorry all for losing his precious harpe, but recovering it would be for later.

Once all his clawgirls recovered.

Especially Vivian, as he hugged her cozy from behind. The ferns around them swayed as gently as the breaths of both girls. Hugging them both so cozy warm and caring, a wonderful reminder of why he must recover his harpe.

And as soon as possible.

In a distance a bonfire cackled, with lots of girlie laughter around it, and the smell of roasted deer reached him. So much like a feast back at the resort, but without the patrons and Aunt Tilda ruining it.

Apparently his clawgirls weren't that worried about the many nasty beasts of Shadow Forest during the day. Not with all their combat experience starting to up their confidence.

Even the caws of crows and ravens weren't as frightening now, but Romeo kept an eye out to make sure none of those crows and ravens had three red beady eyes.

Vivian even moaned happy. Pressing her sultry body against him and purring like the many kitties she loved to keep until Aunt Tilda forced her to get rid of them.

Unlike Fleur—who always kept the cats secret.

Not that Romeo ever tattled on any of the girls for anything.

Even dense stupid him know better than that.

Especially now that the dragon who Juliet said was her dad was perched so nearby that anyone with a working nose could smell him, and his smoky breath.

His chuckles and storytelling ... sigh, at least Romeo was

far away enough to not to hear it well, or else neither Vivian or Azura would get any rest, and boy, did they both need it.

That Azura somehow survived being swatting back here from so far away that they heard her scream and, well, the dragon actually saved her ...

Never mind all those "What a yummy bunny girl!" comments.

Azura was now snoozing and purring against him, as happy as a bunny girl could be. Her long bunny ears were so soft and cozy, he couldn't help but play and stroke them a little bit.

Okay, more than a little bit.

Enough for Azura to purr even more.

Of course, everyone agreed, more like insisted, no more sex until they all were very much safer, not in the middle of Shadow Forest, full of hostile beasts and worse, and so the dragon had agreed he'd be the enforcer of the no-sex till safety policy.

His knowing chuckles ... Romeo really didn't care for what might count as safe enough, but he knew when he was outnumbered.

And no harpe either.

But they'd get it back. That's their next order of business. And stopping whatever that Macker the Cruel plotted. Stop the revival of the baelzog—if that's even what they were really planning.

Fleur even insisted they should first meet up with Veuve Noire and work out what had actually happened between

Romeo, Vivian, and them, and maybe even get help from the other archnofeys as well.

But for now, Juliet was letting him keep her blade.

Even better, everyone, including Vivian and Azura, agreed that Juliet could nap with Romeo this time too. Her little adventure and the fact she was the first lover and blah blah blah, so on his other side, she snoozed against him, him side-hugging her.

Like a dream come true, again.

(Minus the no-sex-for-now policy.)

About the Author

Widely traveled, Jonathan Evan Hudson spends as much time studying life as he does writing gripping tales of fantastic adventures. From the giant redwoods of California to the deserts of Israel, his thrilling stories all draw on first-hand experiences and expand them with the fantastic and his acclaimed creativity.

Be the first to know!
For the updates and more:
www.JonathanEvanHudson.com

youtube.com/@jonathanevanhudson
tiktok.com/@jonathan.evan.hudson

A War Of Lust And Oak

Read Now!

THE ELF GIRL EFFECT

READ NOW!

The acclaimed Jonathan Evan Hudson once again weaves an unforgettable tale brimming with spicy page-turning action and fast-burning enemies-to-lovers passion.

Meet the newly knighted Roo Vorshaya. Sworn to protect humanity in the isolated mountain town of Appleharth. Dreams of action-packed adventure and passionate love under a lovely but sinister strawberry-pink sky.

Love re-ignited by a whiff of the familiar peaches and cream scent of his long-lost childhood girlfriend: the notorious elven witch Amber Peaches.

And endangering everything Roo holds dear.

Love page-turner novels of epic fantasy? Love reading from dusk to dawn? Then go read *The Elf Girl Effect* now!

Martial Art Of The Phantom Saber

Read Now!

Succubus Slash

Read Now!

The acclaimed Jonathan Evan Hudson weaves an unforgettable tale of thrilling action and adventure spiced with fast-burning romance and doused deep in epic fantasy.

Enter Miles Mayhem. Rich in friends and enemies. And a fat boy badass in the sword.

A seriously delicious smell of bacon and eggs smothered in spiced razor-hot cheddar signals celebration—and serious trouble ahead.

Trouble beyond anything Miles ever expected.

The perfect epic fantasy novel. A genre-enlarging feast for fans of sexy action and fabulous adventure. Read *Succubus Slash* now!

Sword Master Of Honey Heart Resort

Read Now!

Into Shadow Forest

A diamond in the rough the bestselling Jonathan Evan Hudson weaves a thrilling tale from explosive beginning to satisfying end in the awe-inspiring land of Grandcrest.

The talented twenty-something sword master Romeo Bladell yearns for love and adventure.

And at the musty edges of Shadow Forest. Near the towering high oaks bearded like stout old dwarves. By a canyon like a wound gnashed deep through in the granite. A canyon like the maw of a stone dragon.

A strange unexpected rope bridge hangs silently. Sinisterly.

Beckoning adventure—and danger unimaginable.

Enter *Into Shadow Forest* and savor the most spectacular of page-turning epic fantasy novels. Love unique monsters, riveting battles, and fantastic femme fatales? Then read *Into Shadow Forest* now!

Angels Of The Sword

Read Now!

Crossing Of Shadowed Death

Read Now!

The acclaimed master of fantasy Jonathan Evan Hudson once again shines through with his talented story-telling. Time to enter another stunning awe-inspiring world of dangerous demons, magical mayhem, and action-packed adventure.

A simple demon-hunting mission. The young and lonely Dirk yearns for amazing adventure, for gorgeously under-dressed dancer girls among the towering high ferns. Among the even taller pines of the hot and humid Fern Shadow Forest.

Pine needles everywhere. And so fragrant they made the finest of teas.

Sturdy reliable cobble roads of the Divine Empire cut through the whole entire forest. Providing the only safe passage.

Or so Dirk thought ...

Enjoy this sexy, action-packed epic fantasy adventure from the talented Jonathan Evan Hudson. Love to read an enthralling epic fantasy novel full of stunning rip-roaring battles with creative new monsters? Then go read *Crossing of Shadowed Death* now!

A Taste of Out of Shadow Forest

The acclaimed bestseller Jonathan Evan Hudson outdid himself once again! He delivers nightmarish foes, deep passion, and amazing action.

High up on a bearded oak tree within Shadow Forest, his back to the mossy trunk, our one-of-a-kind sword master Romeo Bladell yearns for home. For Aunt Tilda's famous peach pies. Her greasy bacon and eggs breakfast. All while the breeze carrying the wonderful almond and vanilla scent of his beloved Velvet Ruins makes him yearn for more time with all his beloveds.

Until a dangerously mysterious rooster cry deep in Shadow Forest.

A new deadly challenge his way.

*Enter **Out of Shadow Forest** and embrace the most thrilling of epic fantasy novels. Perfect for fans of unique monsters, riveting*

CHAPTER 1
ROMEO

Romeo Bladell knew, for sure he knew, that there were absolutely no roosters in the middle of Shadow Forest, and yet that cock-a-doodle-do was no doubt so very rooster-like, wow. It was as loud and proud as any rooster challenging the sun in the morning, a mere bird that was determined to rise higher and brighter than the sun itself.

His back was to a wide mossy trunk of another oak, while he sat knees to chest on an incredibly thick and low winding branch, all hiding among the countless broad leaves.

Alone this time, for now, but the murk around him was more than bright enough for the morning. Plenty of light was sprinkled everywhere like the many, many crumbs of Aunt Tilda's famously delicious peach pies for dessert.

She even insisted that without the countless crumbs it just wouldn't be peach pie.

Just like without sprinkles of sunlight, it just wouldn't be a proper morning in Shadow Forest … kinda.

What Romeo would do for a taste of one of Aunt Tilda's peach pies right now … but she'd smack him silly for yearning for a dessert when it was time for breakfast. Bad enough that cock-a-doodle-do was getting louder and louder.

Closer and closer.

Don't think of a good greasy eggs and bacon breakfast right now. The kind of breakfast both his ma and Aunt Tilda were famous for.

But no doubt the source of the cock-a-doodle-do was on the ground. A good several paces below the very branch Romeo slept on. Every inch and cranny of his body ached but, like pa often said, that was just another way his body let him know he was still very much alive and well, despite whatever beating he took earlier, or, in this case, his makeshift bed helped him survive another night in Shadow Forest and its countless horrors within its endless murk.

That he slept in his red jerkin and brown slacks, sigh. If only he hadn't skipped the shirt so many days ago, but no crying over spilt milk.

Even better, Aunt Tilda wasn't here to wallop him either, for daring to think about spilling some precious milk again.

But ack!

Twigs snapped loud and clear nearby, but behind him. Leaves rustled. Crackled. Ferns got scrapped. The source coming his direction, from behind, and it sounded like it was far bigger than any rooster.

Closer to the size of a wolf.

Maybe bigger.

Thankfully Velvet Ruins let him hold onto one of her precious scimitars. Its curved blade was a wicked lightning violet and yet there was no doubt it was forged from human bone. The lavender handle felt like quality ivory too, but they both knew it was somehow forged from human remains, at least from what Velvet was told. The balance was so perfect, so solid, but not too heavy, not too light, he was still utterly shocked at the scimitar's quality.

Nothing short of the best for a clawgirl like Velvet Ruins.

Well, before clawgirls like her got demoted to fodder slaved to their lessers. Lessers clawgirls used to command themselves.

A fate Romeo saved Velvet from.

Back a few days ago she showed her appreciation by not just fighting beside him, but fighting with him in the gorgeously bare utterly nude to as the sexiest thank you ever.

Well, recently, when his other clawgirl girlfriends insisted Velvet finally let her outfit regenerate from his Puributcher Technique and, ugh, that no-sex-until-safe policy hammered away another joy in life.

But in return Velvet got to guard Romeo for the last few days, and with her velvety voice, she was one fine singer, singing him gently to sleep each and every night.

A cool breeze stirred through the forest, rustling countless leaves, and right into his broad but now scruffy face. It filled his breath with the natural musty earthiness of these woods, and best of all, that strangely natural almond and vanilla musk of the stunningly gorgeous Velvet, who, was hidden by a strategic cluster of broad leaves from all directions except his own.

She was laying down a pace ahead of him, and still snoozing sexy on the very same branch, but unfortunately, now fully dressed. Her violet leotard fit perfectly, with pink hearts in choice places to emphasize her lushest curves.

As in curved perfectly slim in the right spots, and super-heavy in the moneymaking chest spots.

Just like how her fine smooth skin had such an exotically tanned complexion like toasted almonds and was just as sweet on the eyes. While her gorgeous heart of a baby face was framed with long lush black hair that went curly at the bottom, near her shoulder blades, even after she slept sexy sweet for him on her side. Also so that her other scimitar laid above her, strapped to her side facing the sky, easily in reach.

She slept over a nice thick patch of moss, even if she deserved far more than that extra comfort, and not just from all the sexy she offered him these last few days.

Especially after saving him time and time again from hazards he himself missed, to, no doubt, the chagrin of pa and his grandpa.

But while her bright beautifully violet eyes met his, clearly wide and worried, her cherry-lipped grimace was directed downward ... and—

Another cock-a-doodle-do?

Velvet shuttered, eyes shutting. Shivering.

Cringing?

Romeo gasped. Tried to catch her attention again. Ask

what was wrong without speaking the words and revealing their location.

But no.

Velvet started to curl up. As if ... if the very sound of the rooster was hurting her?

And hurting her badly.

CHAPTER 2
ROMEO

No. It couldn't be a rooster.

The rustles below, of leaves being stepped on heavily, crinkling, and the scrapping of many ferns together, snapping more than a few of their stems along the way … no.

It sounded like it was at least as big as a wolf. Maybe bigger.

No rooster was that big.

But then what was it? Romeo never heard of any legend about monsters with rooster-like calls. Or that clawgirls like Velvet had any dislike of roosters. No. Her kind were meant to be able to hide among mankind. Seduce and slay guys like Romeo, but not all clawgirls embraced such a vile lifestyle. More than a few didn't, actually, since a human's lifestyle nowadays, not so bad. It was so good that a number of the gorgeous girls working off their debts at the Honey Heart

Resort run by Aunt Tilda turned out to be clawgirls enjoying their human lifestyle, for the most part, at least.

There was no chance Velvet would be weak against an actual rooster or its call.

If only he could check on his other clawgirl girlfriends, but he wasn't about to leave Velvet here alone and vulnerable.

The twisting limbs full of big broad oak leaves around this winding thick branch hid Romeo from the creature, but also hid the creature form him.

Same for Velvet, who, only a pace away, was curled up like a fetal baby on the thick soft moss and trembling now.

Romeo had to move. To get up. His suede boots were more like suede socks. They'd let him feel the rough bark of the tree.

But that wouldn't stop the bark from crumbling, snapping underneath his movement.

And making a sound when Velvet was so vulnerable ... no. He gripped the ivory-like handle of this precious scimitar. Shifting around to seek a better view of the coming danger.

Wait.

Not a single songbird chirped. Not a single squirrel scampered. The forest was all but silent.

Even Velvet was utterly silent in her cringing pain.

Romeo gnashed his teeth—silently. That clinched it. The small forest critters knew this world better than he did.

Whatever was cock-a-doodling was a dangerous monster.

The branch Romeo and Velvet were on was at least several

paces above the creature, but no telling how high it could jump. If it was a bird-like monster, it might even be able to fly, some, or at least jump high and glide.

Even chickens could jump high and glide.

Well, some breeds of chicken. Especially certain roosters.

How many times had Romeo, back at home as a little young brat chased the chickens until the rooster came and defended them with its cocky proud life and even defeated him more often than not.

Partly because ma would smack him silly if he hurt the chickens too badly. Let along scare them too badly.

But this creature was no farm rooster. Ambush the monster or ... Velvet flicked her foot at him.

Shook her head at him.

Finger over mouth and silently hushed him.

Before cringing in utter agony once again.

He nodded. Hand tight on her scimitar.

When a chuckle ran out below. A very human but sinister chuckle.

And his blood run colder than ice.

WANT MORE?

Go to

WANT MORE?

Go to

www.JonathanEvanHudson.com